Peppino,
Good as Bread

by
Ann Rubino

Illustrated by
Robert Cimbalo

Peppino, Good As Bread

Text copyright © 2014 Ann Rubino

Cover art and Illustrations copyright © 2014 Robert Cimbalo

Copy editing: Tracy Connor

Library of Congress PCN: Pending

Peppino, Good As Bread,/Ann Rubino [illustrated by Robert Cimbalo] – 1st ed.

978-1-942247-00-5

1. Fiction_Historical 2. Children's Fiction

I. Rubino, Ann.

PRINT EDITION

10 9 8 7 6 5 4 3 2 1   Published by www. catree.com in Evanston, IL

For the real "Peppino"
and those who lived to tell their stories.

Chapters

1. March 1943   Page 7
2. Late Spring 1943   Page 21
3. Summer 1943   Page 31
4. September 1943   Page 39
5. Fall 1943   Page 43
6. November 1943   Page 53
7. Winter 1943-44   Page 63
8. December 1943   Page 71
9. January 1944   Page 75
10. February 1944   Page 81
11. Early Spring 1944   Page 87
12. March 1944   Page 93
13. Late Summer 1944   Page 97
14. Late Fall 1944   Page 107
15. Spring 1945   Page 111
16. May 8, 1945   Page 119
17. Summer 1945   Page 125
18. Fall-Winter 1945   Page 133
19. December 1945   Page 137
20. January 1946   Page 143
21. February 1946   Page 145
22. March 1946   Page 153
23. Early April 1946   Page 157
24. Late April 1946   Page 167

Chapter 1
March 1943

As I raced around a corner in the *piazza*
kicking my homemade ball, I crashed into Vituccio,
the *banditore*, town crier, whose shouts echoed off
the stone walls. He was a funny old man with baggy
pants, retired from being a soccer referee, with a
voice that you could hear a mile away. Everybody
called him *Vituccio u'ca caat*, Little Vito poopy pants.
He hated that baby nickname but everybody used it.
Over and over he shouted: "All metals must be turned
in tomorrow in the *piazza*. Pots, pans, even jewelry.
The war effort requires sacrifice. *Il Duce*'s orders." I
saw two police walking our way, looking at me. I had
to keep moving.

"*Scusi*, Vituccio," I said. "I'm late for dinner.
And watch out in back of you..." Bending lower,
Vituccio whispered, breathing his tobacco breath into
my face. "Tell your mother, Peppino. They're serious
this time. The war isn't going well. The police will

be coming house to house! You don't play around
with the government!" He straightened up and kept
shouting, checking over his shoulder from time to
time.

I headed across the little park, and burst into
my house at the end of the street. "I just talked to—"

"I heard it," my mother, Lucia, said. She
reached up to push her dark hair away from her face,
leaving a smudge of flour. She looked worried and
angry. "I have to hide my good pans somehow. I
can't lose everything I've sweated for. They squeeze
us like grapes and we're supposed to be grateful.
After three years of a stupid war we're worse off than
before and now they want my best pans! What do
they think we've been doing?"

"Just hide them, Ma'. Put them in a hole or
something. They can't check every place in town.
Maybe inside a wall."

"You're right! Go find the *muratore*, Giovan'.
Tell him we have an emergency. Say our wall needs
fixing. He'll understand. Don't get caught!"

"The *fascisti* are out there watching, Ma'.
What if they get me? They're right in the *piazza* and
I'll have to go past them."

"Here, I'll give you a note. Say you have to
bring it to your aunt. She's needed to make cheese
tomorrow. Say your mother forgot to tell her. Then
just run. You can get back before curfew."

I'm faster than those bullies, I thought, but
my heart was thumping as I slipped out the side door
and around the corner.

Giovan' arrived just before sundown, carrying
his shovel in his calloused hand, his mason's tools

dragging down the pockets of his dingy jacket. "I hate to break into this wall. I built it to last." But he went right to work, chipping a hole through the soft *tufa* stone wall, and I carried the stone scraps and the dirt outside and scattered them in the garden.

Into the hole went Mamma's beautiful copper, the big pasta pot, the little frying pan for *frittate*, the pans for sauces and a brass *braciere* almost a meter wide. In went a cake pan and a small coffee pot. She added her earrings from her wedding. Any good metal that could be melted down went into that hole. Giovan' filled the wall hurriedly, carefully resetting the stone pieces he had knocked out. "Be quiet in the garden," he warned. "People are listening."

As he put in the last piece, there was a loud knock at the door. Mamma ran up the stairs as Giovan' slopped some whitewash over the patch and shoved a chest in front of it. Her voice carried down the tile-covered stairway. "Oh, nothing's wrong here, Officer. You heard pounding? Yes, I know it's curfew, but we have a leak along the edge of the cistern. My brother-in-law is working on it. Would you like *un caffé*? It's no trouble." She was giving him free coffee? I couldn't believe it.

"Peppino," she called down in a sweet voice. "Stop playing around and bring up some fresh water and some almonds for the officer." Giovan' silently let himself out through the big *portone*, his finger to his lips.

"Forget about all this, Peppino," she said when everyone was gone. "You never saw it, the wall was always here, pretend that Giovan' dug us a hole for a new tree. You don't have to lie. Just act stupid. They

expect children to be stupid, so it won't be hard—act like Cousin Vito."

I could act stupid. That came easy. I didn't mind that. But they scared me, these police and soldiers. Always watching. Ready to shoot. Taking what they wanted. Even Mamma was afraid. I thought nothing could make her afraid, not even the devil. But she was afraid of the police and the soldiers. Now she was acting sweet to someone she hated.

Next morning I watched from behind the curtain as people began carrying their pots to the *piazza*. Some had teary eyes, but they saluted as they passed the police. The children were helping their mothers carry things because most of the fathers were in an army-- either Italian or American. We had men on both sides. Mamma sacrificed one second-best pot as a contribution, to show her cooperation. She saluted like the rest. The mayor's mother carried a beautiful copper *braciere* proudly down the street from her house and laid it on the pile. When the others turned away I saw her slip it under her coat and go home. About an hour later, I saw her go to the *piazza* again—with the same *braciere*—and then pull the same trick. I told Mamma. She made a sour face and said, "Keep watching." The mayor's mother did that trick five times. Nobody stopped her or even raised an eyebrow. The *fascisti* saluted her each time and made a little bow. We worried about the inspectors, but no one ever came to check. It was the bullies' way of getting the metals. It was good to know that Mamma was smarter and more clever than any of them. "Where would I be if I ever lost her?" I thought. "Who would take care of me then?"

Once the bombing started, we moved our rabbits into the basement. I loved those furry rabbits—their cute little pink eyes and fluffy tails. I fed them every day and gave them water, and sometimes I'd sneak them lettuce from our garden.

My grandpa, *Nonno*, came by every day on his way home from the fields, on the way to his house near the *piazza*. He'd stop to rest his bad leg and drop off whatever fresh vegetables he could spare. He'd check to see that we were safe, because *Papá* was in America. I was proud to carry the family name as the first and only son of my *papá*, a big responsibility. I think *Nonno* secretly liked me the best of all his grandchildren.

" Give me a hand here, Peppino," he said one afternoon. He had one of our rabbits out on the big worktable and a sharp knife in his hand. "It's time we ate some meat. Your mother looks pale. Don't you see how thin she is? You hold the back legs tight and don't let him move." I held the rabbit's soft legs as he squirmed and his little claws scratched at my hand.

Nonno quickly slit the rabbit's throat. The blood ran into a drain in the floor. He blew through a slit in the skin to release it. The skin came off inside out like a bloody sock. I couldn't believe it—my kind Grandpa was a rabbit killer! He wiped his hands on his baggy pants, propped his cane against the wall, and sat down on an old chair. I stood there shaking. I didn't know he was going to kill it! I just mumbled, "Why, *Nonno*? Why?"

"That's how nature works," he said. "Nature is harsh and not always the way we would like it. *Cosí è la vita*. That's just how life is." My heart cramped up inside, but there was nothing I could do. I wiped my tears on my rough sleeve.

That night there was meat in the spaghetti sauce for the first time in weeks. I ate plain pasta with a big piece of bread. It was hard to swallow.

Mamma felt my forehead, but there was no fever. She peered into my eyes and made me stick out my tongue. She straightened up and gave me a piercing look. "*Coraggio!* " she said. "Get over it! Have courage! Some live and some die. That's how it is. Be a man! People are dying all over town. You can't cry over a rabbit!"

I sniffled and wiped my nose with my sleeve. "There's too much dying," I cried. Sometimes when I saw planes gliding across the sky—not even bombing, just looking—I wished I could be up there away from all the dying instead of at home hiding from bombs. Just fly up through the clouds, above everybody, safe and free.

We had lambs, too. The German soldiers had counted all the animals in town and kept a careful list. One day a soldier came in when *Nonno* was at our house, and said that he would come back for a lamb when our sheep had her twins. "One for you, one for the army," he said. "You farmers have it too easy! Look how fat she is!" I hid behind a big bag of almonds and listened. The soldier looked fat and well-fed himself, I thought. He ought to know.

"Oh, I don't think so, Sir," *Nonno* protested. "She just drank a lot of water."

The soldier shook his head, patted his big black pistol and sneered, "I'll be back."

Early next Tuesday morning *Nonno* was

staying with us to care for the mother sheep, when I
heard some bleating from the basement, and then a
quiet rustling as *Nonno* limped down the cool marble
steps in his bare feet. I peeked around the corner
in time to see him pick up the newborn lamb, still
wet from being inside the mother, and wrap it in a
piece of old blanket. Out he went to the garden and
hid it under the sticks in the woodpile. You couldn't
see anything there because of all the sticks, and the
lamb was too young to even squeak. Back he came,
and sure enough there was the twin, just born. He
cleaned up the sheep, wiped off the lamb, and it
began to take milk from the mother.

An hour or two later the German officer, the
Leutnant, showed up grinning. "Let's have that
lamb," he said—"I heard some bleating just now as
I was passing by. It will make a nice supper for my
group. Your sheep must have had twins after all."

" Oh, no. She had just this one! See? Here it is.
Please don't take it. We need to eat, too." It broke my
heart to see my kind old *Nonno* beg. The *Leutnant*
looked all around. He peeked behind the shelves
and kicked over some boxes. My heart sank as he
passed the new patch in the wall. I tried to look in
another direction so he wouldn't see my eyes glued
on the patch, but he was focused on getting our lamb.
He stepped in stinky dung and became angry. He
scrubbed it off his boot with some straw from the
rabbit pen, swearing in German.

We stood and watched, not daring to move a
muscle. He finally got tired of grubbing around in the
damp smelly stone basement and said, "Just give me
this one then. She can grow another one later. You
look like you have enough to eat. All you peasants

find stuff to eat. You can eat some weeds. I hear they make good soup." *Nonno* started to object, but the soldier grabbed the new lamb, plopped it across his shoulders and marched out, slamming the door behind him.

After a couple of hours *Nonno* slipped out and got the other lamb and gave it back to the mother sheep. Someday it would give us milk for cheese, and not become some soldiers' *sauerbraten.*

"Soldiers are coming up the street for their eggs," Mamma shouted down to me in the basement a couple of days later. I was changing the goat's damp, sour-smelling straw bedding, carrying it out to the compost pile and bringing in fresh straw. "Go get what we have and hope they'll settle for those!"

The two old brown hens were on their nests in the woodpile, giving me a dirty look whenever I came close. They always pecked me when I took the eggs, and they were learning to go for my eyes. I was waving and hollering, hoping to scare them off the nests when my pal Dominic climbed over the wall, carefully avoiding the chips of glass on top. He let his long legs down and dropped quietly behind the woodpile.

"*Che fai?* What're you doing? You'll just make them cranky so they won't make any more eggs!"

"I have to get eggs and give them to the soldiers," I said. "They said we have to give ten. Otherwise they may beat me up, and hurt Mamma."

"Why do you care about those stupid soldiers," Dominic sneered. "We can fix them good this morning. We'll get ten eggs and stick a pin in the ends. Suck out all the insides."

"That's disgusting!"

"They are not disgusting. They are delicious."

"You are really crazy! Just like Mamma says."

"No, listen. We can do this. Just try one, like this, with a pin. That's it! Make a tiny hole in each end."

I did. It was slimy. We each sucked out five. I was getting full. "Now what?" I said. "They still want those eggs and now they're too light."

"That's the beauty of it, Peppino. Here, hold them down in the water bucket. See? They fill up. You can see the bubbles. They'll be heavy again. We'll give them the sack of eggs with a nice little bow, and they'll be added to all the other eggs. Nobody will know which ones they were."

I admired Dominic's nerve. He'd tell anybody off, even if they were going to shoot him or beat him like his mean father did. He could outwit anybody.

We held the shells down in a bucket of water that we dipped out of the *pozzo* until no more bubbles came up. We laid them neatly in a sack. When the soldiers came around with a cart collecting all the eggs, we tenderly put the eggs in their pile, gently moving some around so they wouldn't roll. We saluted politely and watched as they made their way down the street, stopping at every house that had chickens. They checked them all off on their chicken-count list.

Mamma came around the corner of the garden. "What's going on here? You two look far too cheerful. Are you pleased to see our food taken away down the street?"

Dominic and I couldn't stop our giggles then. "We

gave them empties, Ma'! We sucked out the insides first. We cheated them and got away with it. They're not as smart as they think they are."

"You what? You're crazy. If they ever find out who did it they can burn our house down! These pranks of yours are dangerous!"

"They'll never know, *Signora*," Dominic said. "All the eggs from this street are in one big basket, and they won't burn down the whole street. They steal their food from us. We're like a big food market to them. Didn't they take your baby lamb? And your other five chickens?"

"They did, and they carry guns, too," Mamma said. "They're not afraid to use them either. You do tricks once too often and that will be the end of us."

Dominic wouldn't give in, though. "When they came to claim our eggs last week my father told them to come every night and feel inside the chicken to see if it really has an egg. Then tell us how many to give. The stupid soldier started to reach for his pistol, but then my father said, 'Who will raise your food if you kill us all?' I guess that made him think. He put his gun back, spit on our floor and marched out."

Mamma looked doubtful. I didn't know what to say, caught between Mamma's fear and Dominic's daring. "Didn't they come around and check if you have any big bags of flour in your shed?" Dominic went on. "Anyway I'm not afraid. Soon the Americans will come and kick their butts out of here."

Dominic always talked tough, just like his father but not as mean. The soldiers scared me, though. I'd seen them shoot a man who talked back to them. They just put the gun up to his head and shot him and walked away leaving him in the street like garbage. But hearing Dominic made me feel braver.

Later that day Mamma's friend Angelina came hobbling up out of breath to the door, and grabbed Mamma by the arm. "Somebody tricked the soldiers," she said, hiding her toothless mouth behind her hand. Her curved back shook with laughter. "When they came to collect he gave them eggs filled with water. All the insides had been sucked out. *Che coglioni!* What a nerve! He could have been shot! I passed by headquarters just now. The *Kommandant* was shouting at the egg collecting team. 'You will be punished for this! You could be sent to the Russian front! How could you be so naïve, tricked by ignorant peasants? Eggs full of water? Nobody in town has flour? All the sausage and wine have disappeared? You are too stupid to see beyond your boots!' "

"We may not be *istruiti*, with lots of schooling, Angelina," Mamma said. "But we're not going to starve on our own land. Maybe that's what the four soldiers were doing, marching up and down with heavy packs on and sour faces. Good for them that they get in trouble. Let's just hope they don't think to look in the cistern where the sausage is hidden..." She bit her lips to keep from smiling.

Chapter 2
Late Spring 1943

A few weeks after the bombing had been going on, a man showed up at our front door in a good suit, freshly pressed. His shoes were shined. There was a bright white handkerchief in his top pocket and he wore a smooth rounded hat. He smelled like spice or perfume, not rabbit bedding. He was definitely not one of us. He must have had servants to keep him looking so neat.

"Good Morning, *Signora*," he said as Mamma opened the door. "I am the mayor's personal assistant, Giorgio Tapella. The mayor has decided to move into town here, away from Bari. The raids on the city have become more dangerous, and besides he wants to help protect his mother who lives here."

"What a nice son," said Mamma narrowing her eyes. " *Che buon figlio....cosi bravo*. He respects his mother, how nice. Why are you telling this to me?

She has a large house of her own." She raised her chin skeptically.

"Your house has been chosen for him to use," he replied. "It is the best house in this neighborhood and there are only the two of you, what with your husband away in America." He wiggled his eyebrows and gave us a look to show that he knew that *Papá* was living among the enemy.

"His mother has a very nice villa, with palm trees and rhododendrons, just at the end of this street. People call her *'Margarit' d' u'casin'* because of her fancy house," Mamma argued. "She's only one person. The lovely garden has a wall and an iron gate, *un cancello,* with a lock. She could use the company and he'd be close to his office in the *municipio.*"

"It is not your decision, *Signora,*" he said, pulling himself up as tall as he could and frowning. "The mayor wants to live here, not with his mother. After all, he's a grown man, an official, a person of stature. He can't live with his mother like a boy. In any case, it has been decided. In two days he and his wife will come to live in this house. He will allow you to stay here, on the lower level, in your storage." Mamma started to protest, but she couldn't get a word out. "Bring your bed and clothing down to the storage," he continued. "There's a fireplace and you'll be close to the *pozzo* for your water. You may continue to use the roof for hanging washing and drying food. The mayor's family will take care of your possessions. Perhaps your friends will help you move downstairs. *Buon giorno.*" Off he went, shiny shoes squeaking, to report to the mayor that all had been taken care of.

Mamma closed the door hard and sputtered. She said a lot of words I hadn't heard before. She slammed her fist against the inside of the heavy door and cried. She put her finger sideways against her mouth and bit it. I had never seen Mamma cry, not even when she cut her finger. Not even when *Papá's* letters from America didn't come anymore. But we were too scared to resist. The Fascists controlled everybody. Talking back could mean jail. If we defied the Nazis we could be shot. Any time we spotted soldiers or police we saluted with our arm in the air and then got out of the way. How I hated them!

Finally she took a deep breath, wiped her dark eyes on her apron and told me, "Let's get going. Uncle Luigi will help carry the bed and table down. Get your clothes together into a sack and bring them down. We'll live like Gypsies with our cart and our stored almonds and our hidden pots and our animals. We can move back up once that arrogant good-for-nothing piece of dirt moves back to Bari. Be sure to bring down our *braciere* to keep us warm. He won't need that. We know he has a good one!"

That same day we carried our stuff down stairs to the lower level that served as a garage for our farm equipment—stone floor, no decorations, two small windows high up. A thin wood divider at one end formed a closet for almonds after harvest. A large door, the *portone,* was wide enough to drive a horse and cart inside.

A door at the other side led into the actual basement, under the main house. Rabbits had their pen down there. We had a goat there, too, for milk. We changed the straw every day, but everything we had smelled like a barn.

The chickens lived in the garden, and laid their eggs between the sticks and pieces of wood. My job was to find the eggs every morning and bring them in. The fireplace burned wood, or charcoal if we could get it. Mamma broiled pieces of meat or fish over the fire and cooked everything else in a big pot that hung on a bracket. There was no sink, no bathroom. Clean water came up in a bucket from the *pozzo*. Dirty water went into a sewer hole in the garden, food scraps and peelings went into the compost, and anything burnable was saved in the woodpile along with the branches and pruning scraps.

We didn't ever have leftovers. Cooking was hard for Mamma, carrying water for everything she did. When it was cold we built a little fire in the *braciere* and sat around it with our feet up on the rim. We hung up a curtain at one end to make a bedroom, and put the table near the fireplace to form the kitchen. Our smelly chamber pot was off in the corner.

Often we used candles to save our one electric light that hung from the ceiling. I did my schoolwork there on an old table, until the schools closed completely. Mamma brought her sewing over at night to keep me company, share the light and give me math lessons. We kept a black curtain over our little window so bombers wouldn't see our lights.

Mamma's lessons were different from the teacher's. She only had fourth grade herself, so she taught me the math she used to shop and manage the fields. She gave me problems to figure out. "You have 5 kilograms of almonds, and sell them for 5 *lire* each.

How much should you get?" "If I spend 250 *lire* on 100 rooted grape cuttings, how much did each one cost me? If each one then produces 4 kilograms of grapes and I sell them for 3 *lire* each, do I make any money for my work?" At first I worked them out on scraps of paper with a pencil, mumbling the number facts to myself. Later when I could do them in my head, I liked to show off. "How much do you make per kilo of almonds if the price goes up 10%," she'd call out, and I'd shoot back the answer. *Nonno* would clap and then she'd shoot a question at each of my cousins. Those contests were fun and I usually won.

When I was small, before the bombing, she let me help sell our crops. The buyers carried the heavy olives in baskets to be weighed. They hung the baskets on one end of a big balance scale; iron weights were on the other. Sometimes one would put his foot under the edge of the basket to make it lighter to pay less.

My job was to bend down and watch. I'd shout "The foot, Mamma! The foot!" One time a buyer hit me for shouting. Mamma had her pruning knife out in a flash. "You touch my son again, you'll regret it!" He backed up so fast he knocked over a basket of olives and they rolled all over.

"We will add the cost of that basket to your bill," she said, lifting up her chin and narrowing her eyes at him. "Think of the price next time you want to push people around." They weren't ashamed to cheat. They were just ashamed to be found out. Mamma and I were a tough team to beat, a tough team to cheat.

Two days after we moved downstairs, the

Mayor came with his stuck-up wife, and movers carried up loads of clothes, books, food, and plenty of pots. I spotted one mover carrying a big copper *braciere* almost a meter wide, even shinier than the one that his mother had given to the war five times over. We watched through the small windows and hoped they'd trip over their stuff, but they were quite sure-footed.

"*Che faccia tosta*," Mamma muttered. "What a 'hard face'—moving into a person's house without even an 'Excuse me!' They didn't even say 'hello.' It is as if we don't exist. We're just down here under their feet and that's where they think we belong. Well, once the war is done and the Americans win, we'll see how proud they feel!"

Shortly after the move, Mamma spotted the *podestá*, the mayor, in the *piazza*. "*Don* Flavio, *un momento per favore*," she said, tapping him on his wide red, green and white sash of office. Giorgio, his assistant, grabbed her sleeve to pull her away. "I need to talk to you a minute."

"I'm a busy man," the mayor said, waving his cigar. "Don't bother me. I'm on the way to a meeting with the *Kommandant*."

"*Don* Flavio, you've taken over my house," Mamma insisted. "You've ordered me to move my family into the storage area. I'm cooking on a fireplace and sleeping with rabbits and goats. You owe me a minute!"

"*Avete ragione, Signora*. You make a good point. Let her talk, Giorgio." He waved him away.

"This morning workers showed up at the house and started breaking into my walls in two

places. They put a cart full of building stones and a
load of copper pipes against my garden gate. What
are they doing to my house?"

" An improvement, courtesy of the Italian government. They're building a bathroom with its own
toilet and putting a water pipe into the kitchen as
well. You're lucky. This is a very expensive improvement. You know Mussolini always tries to improve
the lives of the Italian people. Fresh water from the
fountains, free schools, trains run on time. Always
progress. Always forward. Now I really must go."

"*Buon lavoro, Don* Flavio. I wish you
happy work. Just don't work too hard, helping the
Kommandant. " The look she gave at his back could
have melted him down into a puddle.

After the remodeling was done, we could hear
them walking around above us but after a while we
got used to it. Whenever I heard the water flushing
down the pipe past my bed, it made me mad that I
was still peeing in a pot to be emptied in the garden.
It was hard for Mamma to carry water up from the
pozzo for washing. Not to speak of walking to the
fountain in the *piazza* every day for a bucket of clean
drinking water.

But at least it will be left behind for us later,
we told ourselves. Once the Americans come.

Giovan' cut another door into the ground level
so we didn't have to open up the big *portone* to go
in or out. That smaller new door led out to the stairway up to the roof, and it was a quick way out to the
street. It helped in the winter when the cold, damp
wind blew every day. I learned to put my shoes on
before getting out of bed, and then my pants, because

of that cold stone floor. I ripped my pants sometimes but I didn't freeze my feet.

The mayor and his wife acted as if no one was living under their feet. They'd go proudly in and out of the big front door as if they owned the place. They never came downstairs or even into the garden. Maybe they thought we'd make them help with the work. Even in the street, they never said hello.

Chapter 3
Summer 1943

One night I heard a loud boom—like huge
firecrackers—and then people outside my window
began shouting. "Run and hide! The planes are dropping bombs! *Maledetta l'America! Che scemi!* Cursed
Americans! What fools! Why do they want to hurt
us?" I heard a lot of running around outside, and
then it stopped.

"It's over. Go back to bed," Mamma said, and
so we did, sleeping in all our clothes on her big wide
bed. Only a couple of walls had been broken down
the street, and no one was hurt.

It happened again a couple of nights later, and
then again on the weekend. It was the Americans all
right, aiming for the big town, Bari, and they missed.
Nonno told me they were trying to stop the seaport
from being used to ship soldiers and weapons, and

we were only a couple of miles from there. If they could get the Germans to leave, they'd have a good harbor for their ships. But their aim wasn't very good.

"Tonight if the bombers come, we'll run to *Commar'* Angelina's house and hide in her basement," Mamma said. "Those bombs are getting too close for comfort. She has the deepest basement and her walls are extra strong. Unless a bomb hits smack in her *salotto*, we'll be safe."

That night when we heard the airplanes, we jumped out of bed, ran to Angelina's and hid in the basement. All the other women and children were there too, praying. They said the same prayer over and over again until I got a headache. One bomb hit close, breaking part of our garden wall.

A week later the group gathered at the pharmacist's house next door to us and huddled in the corners where the walls were thickest. A bomb hit close, popping his heavy door in. "Run for your lives, but keep down," shouted the pharmacist. We all ran out and lay flat on the ground in the garden. I thought then: How can the blasted planes see us in the dark garden? And do they really care? They're after the army, not a bunch of dumb people lying in a garden! We could smell the explosives and the charred wood all around. Once the planes left, we went home and tried to sleep, but my eyes wouldn't stay closed.

We did the same thing every night for over a week and I was getting really sick of it. Who cares about the boats anyway? Why do they drop bombs on farms if they're after the boats? Their bad aim was

causing a lot of trouble. I didn't see how adults could
be so stupid.

One morning a peddler came into town in a
horse cart with a box full of rosaries. He came up
to our small door and knocked as I was feeding the
lamb. Mamma went to the door.

"These rosaries are specially blessed, *Signora*.
They come in many lovely colors and they always
work. It is a very small investment. They are guar-
anteed to bring the war to an end. See, here, try it in
your hand. Don't you feel safer already? Just make
me an offer. I can see you are a holy person and pos-
sibly your husband is in danger." He peered past her
in the doorway, stretching his scrawny neck to see
what we had inside. " Is he at home? Or perhaps you
are a person who makes your own decisions?" He
smiled an oily smile, a sneaky gleam in his eye. He
smelled like tobacco and sweat, and I didn't like the
way he looked at Mamma. She was pretty all right,
but we had *Papá*. But I needn't have worried. She
wasn't fooled. Mamma told him to go stuff his rosaries. He went off in a huff. I thought he hit his tired
horse extra hard.

That night in the basement, a lot of Mamma's
friends had new rosaries and we tried them out.
We were all scared stiff by now. We were willing to
try anything. Over and over I heard: "*Ave Maria!
Misericordia!*" I don't know if God could hear us over
the noise. It was good business for the peddler, but
the bombing went on.

One night as we ran to the shelter, we saw
Michelina, our neighbor, up on her flat roof watching all the explosions. Up where she hung her washed

clothes and dried her tomatoes, she had brought out a wooden kitchen chair and was sitting watching the fire show. She had curly yellow hair. "From a bottle," Mamma said. The pilots could probably see her bright hair from the air. I knew she was a big fireworks fan like me, so I wanted to stay and watch. "Can I stay, Mamma? If we see a plane I'll lie down flat."

Mamma grabbed my ear and dragged me on to Angelina's to hide in her basement with the praying team. "You've got to be crazy," she said as we walked, "or stupid. People are getting killed. It isn't a show. It's a war."

After a few weeks, I was getting tired of sleeping in my clothes and running out in the night to pray. "I'm not going!" I shouted one night when the sirens sounded. "I don't care if I die here. I'm tired. I'm sick of the stupid praying and hiding. Leave me alone!"

Mamma wasn't sure whether to smack me or not. I was too big to pick up, and we could hear the explosions starting. She gave me a long, thoughtful look and said, "All right. Your choice. I hope you make it. I'm going." And she went. If my *Papá* was here, he would have stayed so I wouldn't be alone, I thought. He'd understand how sick I am of this stupid war.

The next morning we woke up to *Commar'* Michelina pounding on the door, her curls bouncing up and down, screaming outside. "They've bombed Sannicandro! I was watching the fireworks last night..." Tears of worry ran down her face and her lipstick was crooked.

"*Si. Tu sei pazza!* Crazy! They're not fireworks! They're bombs!" Mamma said as she opened
the door and pulled her inside. "And what's that on
your face? You should be ashamed, painting yourself
with your husband away."

"I was watching, don't stop me, and I saw a lot
of explosions and fires off in that direction, near the
water supply. My husband's cousins live there! We
have to go and help!"

"We'll go right now. Get your clothes on,
Peppino! Don't mess around. Grab your sweater."
Out we went with me hobbling in my untied shoes,
hitching up my short pants as I ran. We hurried out
of town and past the olive fields. I was ahead of them
by the time we reached the next town, about five kilometers away. People were filling the dusty road, all
rushing in the same direction. I wanted be one of the
first to discover what happened.

As I got close to the town, I could see big
smoking holes in the ground where the bombs had
hit. Houses were still burning. A terrible smell hit
me like a punch in the belly—the sweet sick smell of
dead things. We saw dead bodies in the church lined
up under sheets all the way down the long center
aisle, more than I could imagine. I never saw so
many people crying and screaming. Families were
going down the row lifting the ends of the sheets to
find out who had died, and crying and fainting when
they found one they knew. Some of the dead people
were in pieces, put together to make up a whole body.
I ran outside and threw up. Mamma and Michelina
put handkerchiefs over their faces and went down the
whole row, checking for relatives.

They didn't find any of our family, so we headed for home. I was glad that our town didn't have anything worth bombing on purpose. Even a stupid American flier could tell an olive farm from a bunch of boats! We walked a lot slower going back.

As we passed some of our own land, farms are all split into different pieces of land, I saw the fields were filled with rocks that had been blasted out. "All the trees are broken, Mamma! Look at that olive. It's split down the middle. There are branches and rocks all over the place. Look at the big holes... How can we ever get all those stones out to grow the crops? The farm is all ruined!"

But Mamma had a plan. The very next week she got some friends and hired men to add those rocks to the low walls all around the property. The *muratore*, Giovan', was the boss and gave us each a job. My cousin Vito, my friend Dominic and I picked up the middle-sized rocks and put them in Nicola's cart. He brought them to the men who built them onto the wall.

"When do we have lunch, Giovan'? I'm sick of this! It's too hot out here in the sun! I'm hungry and every time I pass the lunch baskets I smell those olives and bread. It's making my stomach growl. "

" What are you, a man or a baby? Do you think the rocks are going to carry themselves? Just keep working. You are strong enough to chase balls and run up and down between the trees. Now you can put some of that energy to work and help out! Just get a drink of water or wine and then get back to those rocks."

By the end of the week, we had built the wall

higher all around. I was tired and sore, but when
I looked at my hands they looked tougher—like a
man's hands. After the first sore-muscle day, I felt
stronger, too. And when we were done, Giovan'
shook my hand with his big rough grip instead of
patting me on the head as he used to.

Two nights later though, when the sirens
sounded and Mamma shook me awake to go hide and
pray, I went—and I prayed.

Chapter 4
September 1943

All the bells started ringing early one morning in September. Clang, clang, bong, bong. The bells rang in all six churches in the little town. It couldn't be another air raid. They never bombed in the mornings.

Commar' Angelina was already pounding on the door with her cane and I heard her chattering to Mamma. "Italy has signed a peace with America! We're not fighting America any more! No more bombing! No more fighting!" She was so excited she was almost spitting the words as her whiskery chin bobbed up and down. Her long black dress was buttoned crooked and one of her black socks drooped down around her slipper.

"You mean the Nazis and Fascists have given up?"

"Not Germany. Just Italy. The news came on Antonio's radio. Italy isn't going to fight America any more. It isn't worth it. They're stronger." Her voice shook with excitement and her hair was starting to poke out of its knot at the back. Her hand trembled on her cane.

"Then the Germans can move out," said Mamma. "Good riddance. We can keep our own animals and crops for a change."

All day long, people were feeling good, but when we looked around, the Germans were still there and the mayor was still in charge, strutting around in the *piazza* wearing his official sash. People were going in and out of his big office in the *municipio* as if nothing had happened.

I found Dominic in the middle of the *piazza*. "What's going to happen, do you think? Are we done with all this fighting? Have you heard anything?" I always asked him about things like this. He was older. He knew how to get things done, how to find out stuff and get what he needed. He had a house and a family but he didn't go there much. There was too much going on in the streets to waste time in a house, he said. Dominic wasn't afraid of anything, not even *fascisti*.

"I don't trust any of them," Dominic said. "They're too mean to quit so easy. The mayor is over at the headquarters now and they're all putting their heads together to make plans. I saw a bunch of officers going into the *municipio*. They didn't look happy. I started to ask one what was going on and he swung his rifle butt at me. I only jumped out of the way in time."

Nobody with good sense would ask Nazis what was happening, only Dominic. He was taller than me, and skinny, with floppy dark hair that he combed with his fingers. He could outrun anyone and his hand-me-down pants with his father's belt flopping didn't slow him down. He was always hanging around the *piazza*, playing ball with any boy that came by and keeping an eye on all the soldiers' comings and goings.

I was worried. What would happen now if we weren't on the side of the Germans? They were still here and in a bad mood. Suddenly we were their enemies, and they had all the guns. My heart went down to my knees. They could do anything to us that they wanted to and we had no way to fight back. What if they just decided to stay? It didn't seem like such good news after all.

Chapter 5

Fall 1943

Voices drifted down to me as I was starting to fall asleep. "This place is disgusting, Flavio! There is dust everywhere since they put in the water pipes and the bathroom. They chipped the plaster and left the pieces! I have to cook every day and there is no one to help me wash the clothes! My fingernails are breaking! We have to do something or I shall lose my mind..."

"Patience, *cara*. We'll get some help for you soon. Your delicate hands won't suffer any more."

"Well, you'd better do something. This is no life for a well-born lady. Living in this godforsaken village! My mother warned me not to marry a politician. Now you see what I have to endure!"

"You'll be pleased to hear this, then. Borgati called me at the office today."

"Borgati? The jeweler? He called all the way

from Rome? What can he want? To sell me more gold
to decorate my dishpan hands?"

"No, no *carissima*. Don't feel bitter. Your
hands are still beautiful. But things are bad in Rome.
Some shops near his were destroyed. People were
rounded up and taken away. Nobody knows where
they went."

I was getting a sick feeling just listening to all
this mush. People are being killed and all her high-
ness cares about are her fingernails.

He continued. "He has an employee who
wants to move out of the city, move to a smaller
town."

"But why would anyone want to move here,
of all places? It's dusty. It's hard to find fresh food.
There are no servants. And now Italy has surren-
dered to the Americans so we don't know what side
we're on! The people here speak a strange kind of
Italian that one can barely understand and they give
me dirty looks when I pass them in the *piazza*. I
think they charge me too much, too. You should see
what I have to pay for an egg!"

"*Cara*, listen to me. We owe Borgati a favor.
He has given you very good discounts on your
jewelry. This woman wants to move out of Rome,
really needs to move away and find other work in
a smaller city. The Fascists will win out, you'll see.
This peace nonsense is only temporary. Things will
get back to normal, but meanwhile you'll have some
help."

"I cannot believe this. The woman wants to
move out of the most beautiful city in the world,
the home of the Pope, the place where the Roman

Emperors lived? Leave Rome and come here to a
place where the biggest monument is an old fort? She
must be insane!"

"Insane or not, she's willing to come here and
work for us as a maid. She can cook and do the dishes
and wash. She works cheaper than your other maid,
free in fact. And you can spare your beautiful hands."

I heard a kiss and a little giggle, ugh, disgusting grownups.

"All right, Flavio. If you insist. If Borgati sends
her she must be honest. Otherwise he'd never keep
her in his jewelry store handling his gold and his
accounts. And she's *romana* like me. I'll take her. We
can set up a small bed for her. She can sleep here in
the kitchen."

Now, we'll have another person in our house,
I thought—a dish-washing jewelry lady. Between
bombs and extra people and countries changing
sides, life is getting to be crazy. And why did she want
to move away in such a hurry?

A few days later I was getting some kindling
from the woodpile in the garden for the fireplace and
was surprised to see a young woman on the other
side doing the same thing. She was tall and thin with
light brown hair tucked under a scarf. Her dress
looked like a teacher's dress, but was covered by a
denim farm apron. Her eyes were sad behind her
wire-rimmed glasses. She reminded me of the beautiful queen in the movie, Genoveffa. All the boys were
in love with that queen, doomed by a jealous enemy
to live in the forest. I was in love with Genoveffa, too.

"What are you doing here? This is our garden
and this is our fire wood." I was very firm, very much

the man of the house. I'd be strong but kind.

"I'm *la serva*. I live here." She pointed to our house, upstairs. "*Donna* Livia wants some wood to burn in her *braciere*. She says it's too cold in her bedroom."

"Are you the one from Rome?" I said. "The one who will work cheaper? The jewelry person?"

Her eyes got big and round and filled with tears. She put her hand on my shoulder. "They'll kill me. Please don't betray me." She sounded desperate and it didn't make any sense to me. It was only a few sticks. We could get more.

"That's all right," I said. "You can have the wood for free. You're not in trouble. I won't tell anybody."

A shout from the upstairs window made us both freeze. "Hurry up with that wood. I'm freezing in here while you take your sweet time! Get a move on!"

"It isn't the wood," the woman whispered. "Nobody must know I'm here from Rome, not the Fascists and especially not the Germans. Promise you won't tell. I only got this job to have a safe place to live."

I rushed inside to tell Mamma about our new person. She must have been sleeping the other night because she was really surprised and wanted to know every word. When I got to the "don't betray" part, Mamma got very still and let out a long breath. "She's right. We need to keep quiet about her for everyone's sake." That didn't make sense. Betray a person over some borrowed sticks? I didn't understand.

That afternoon I was up on the roof while

Mamma was putting out some wash and the new
lady came up with the mayor's freshly washed long
underwear to hang up. Mamma went over to her and
I could just barely hear her whispering.

"Where are you from?"

"Rome."

"What part?"

"Near the river. "

"Near the Pope? Right across the river from
him?"

The voices got even softer. "*Si.*"

Mamma got very quiet again, just as she had
with me. There was a moment of silence. She took a
couple of deep breaths. "I heard that neighborhood
was wrecked by the Nazis. They broke into shops
and homes, and took people away in trucks. No one
knows why."

"Yes. I was up early and saw them coming
in. They started breaking into houses and smashing
windows. They broke into my fiancé's bookstore and
threw the books out into the street." I saw tears piling
up in her eyes, and she slipped the edge of her apron
up under her glasses to blot them.

"You saw this? You were there?"

"Yes. They were pulling people out of the
houses, hitting them with guns, and shoving them
into lines. I couldn't see if Primo was in the line, or
maybe still sleeping above his shop. I couldn't get
near."

"How did you get away?"

"I slipped out through a passageway and ran
to the jewelry shop where I work. There was no time
to take anything or help anyone. My boss let me hide

upstairs. His wife loaned me clothes and brought food to me every day. He found this job for me. *Don* Silvestro, your priest, met me at the train and brought me here on the bus."

"*Poverella*! Don't say too much around here. The mayor is a Fascist bastard, but he's a human being. I don't think he would betray you. He actually may know more than you think. *Donna* Livia, on the other hand, I wouldn't trust her with a bucket of slops."

Mamma took her rosary out of her apron pocket. "Here, take this. Come and hide with us the next time bombers come. You don't have to pray, but the walls are strong and it's good to be with other women. We have to stick together, with the men either gone to the army or old. I can always get another rosary. The salesman comes every month."

"But I don't pray that way."

"Pray any way you like, God doesn't care, but carry this where it can be seen and keep your head down. What is your name?"

"Rachel...Levi. But your priest says I should change it to Rosa Lucci."

"*Don* Silvestro's suggestion is good. You should listen to his advice. You can trust him. Rosa Lucci is a good name. It sounds safer. Say you're from the suburbs of Rome, getting over the loss of your beloved, a lieutenant in the Italian army. If we're making up stories, might as well make them believable. That will explain why you cry often and don't want to talk to people. The less you talk, the better. Your accent is very different. Besides, when you lie a lot, it's hard to remember what you said to whom."

"Why did you tell her to lie, Mamma?" I asked afterwards. "Lying is a sin, *Don* Silvestro says."

"There are worse sins, Peppino, a lot worse. The Nazis are determined to kill all the Jews, in every country where they have power. Even in Italy they have given orders for Jews to report to them and go into camps. Anyone who protects them can be sent to the camps, too. I've heard that they kill the people in these camps. Just plain people, not criminals. Children, even."

"Nice people like Rachel? That's crazy! Why would they kill somebody like her? You can't just kill people for no reason."

"That's what I've heard. *Don* Silvestro knows people who give them a home and a new name until the war is over and the Germans are gone. Changing a name isn't much of a lie to save a person's life. Call her Rosa and keep your mouth closed."

"Just be stupid again, right?"

"What people don't know, they can't repeat. Just don't talk about it. From now on she's Rosa." The next morning I was up on the roof pretending to be studying. I heard *Donna* Livia's voice coming up through the kitchen window.

"Rosa! Where's your ration book? I'm going to the market today."

"I lost it on the way here from Rome." Her voice was quiet. She sounded so polite with that accent.

"You LOST it?" *Donna* Livia shrieked. " Your tickets for food? Your identity card that you have to carry at all times? How stupid can you be? Am I your mother that I have to feed you, too? That's what I get for allowing a stranger into my house." The Roman accent didn't sound so polite, coming from her.

The mayor interrupted. "Now, now, Livia. Don't be upset. Can't you see the girl has had a hard trip? People bring presents all the time to my office, I just have to ask for what I want. We never go hungry here."

"I don't see why we have to provide for another mouth, and a stranger at that," Livia pouted.

"Here, let me shop today," he said. "Give me a list and I'll see that the proper gifts arrive. In fact, I'll get Giorgio to deliver them this afternoon." *Don* Flavio tucked the list in his pocket, went down the stairs and off towards his office as Livia sniffed into her lace-trimmed handkerchief.

I went down around the side of the house and found Mamma inside washing clothes in a bucket. I told her what I had heard.

"Don't worry. *Don* Silvestro has learned a few things in his sixty-three years. I think I'll go over and pray for *Papá* a little."

Later that night there was a soft knock on our small door. It was *Don* Silvestro. He blended with the shadows in his long black coat and flat black hat. He put his finger up for quiet as I let him in. "I found the new girl's documents, Lucia. They were near the bus stop, under some leaves, see? Only a little damp with a bit of mud that can be wiped off, but be careful. Don't smear the ink."

"That's amazing, Father, just when we were starting to look for them. Unbelievable, in fact."

"Yes, the ways of the Lord surpass under-standing." He pointed down at the damp and spotted

papers. "And notice, her name is nice and clear—
Lucci, Rosa; Residenza, Roma. There's an official
Roman stamp on the front and the signature of the
supervisor there." I peered around his elbow. The ink
looked new.

"You want me to give them to her? Why me?"

"So you can truthfully say that I told you I
found them and didn't want to wake the family up.
She'll understand about the 'finding'. Many things
are lost and found in war. Names, documents,
people."

"Yes, Father, I know all about that, unfor-
tunately." I was jumping up and down with
excitement. "Wow, a miracle, I have to tell."

Mamma put a firm hand on my shoulder.
'Hush, *zitto! ZITTO!!* You're not telling anybody, is
that clear? Remember what I told you this morning.
Not a word to anyone. There are miracles that are
best kept silent. This is one of them."

That's when I realized that sheltering Rachel
could bring the soldiers down on all of us. Mamma
knew the Nazis were putting Jewish people on trains
and shipping them away someplace. Rachel must
have run away from them. I'd be silent, all right. I
was too scared to say anything at all.

Chapter 6
November 1943

That was Wednesday, and on Friday when I was waiting with my bucket for a turn at the drinking water fountain, I heard a couple of women talking.

"Did you notice that new maid of the mayor's?" one of them said. "She doesn't look like she's from around here, too tall and thin. And her words sound funny. She wears a nice dress under her apron, too. Why would a maid have such a good dress? Maybe she had a better life before."

The fatter one finished filling her bucket and straightened up. "I heard she's from Rome. A lot of people are leaving there, Jews mostly. The Nazis wrecked their neighborhood, the ghetto. A lot of homes and shops were wrecked. They broke all the windows and burned some bookshops. They said people were taken away."

"Yes, those Nazi thugs are trouble

everywhere—mean and vicious." The lady crossed herself and looked around. "I hope the *americani* hurry up and clear them out."

"*State zitta!* Hush! Don't talk like that! If the Germans hear you, you're dead."

"No. They're not around just now. They're practicing with their guns over at the *Campo Sportivo*."

"Not much sports there now. The ground is muddy and dug up by the machinery. Boys have to play soccer in the streets."

"Well, Jewish or not she'll have to be a saint to put up with that *strega* of a wife *Don* Flavio has. He's OK for a Fascist, not as harsh as most of them, but she's a real witch."

Naturally, I reported all this to Mamma, who looked pretty worried. "You know they could kill us all, don't you? If they really wanted to. Italians don't follow all those regulations of the Nazis, but we shouldn't press our luck. I'll have to have a word with Angelina *ficcanaso* and plant some ideas in her head."

After Mass on Sunday, as we were coming down the church steps, *Commar'* Michelina bustled over, her eyes sparkling. "You'll never believe what I heard about the mayor's new maid. Carmela told me she studied at the Vatican. That's why her Italian is so clear and educated. Angelina told her. I don't know how she knows everything, but it seems that the maid has taken a vow of silence since her fiancé died in the war." She kept on babbling like an over-flowing fountain. "It's so tragic, such a lovely person, but really a *donna seria*, a serious woman to pray

for her beloved like that. And she always carries her
rosary. What a saint."

"She'd have to be one to put up with *Donna*
Livia." Mamma remarked tartly. "But she seems
to be a nice girl. Tell me, were you able to find any
decent dressmaking cloth when you went to Bari? I
need to repair this dress soon." The topic of Rosa was
dropped.

We heard a motorcycle drive up that night
and stop outside. Then we heard heavy steps, the
front door opened and closed, then quiet voices, not
the mayor's. Mamma and Rosa looked up from their
mending, eyes wide and wary. We heard footsteps
above, and the rattle of coffee cups. "Rosa, come
up here!" *Donna* Livia shouted down the stairway.
In one swift movement, Mamma grabbed her jacket
and a couple of shawls and shoved them into Rosa's
hands. She motioned to me with her head to go
toward the stairs, and crept quickly toward the small
outer door, pulling Rosa after her.

"Rosa," *Donna* Livia shouted again. "Do I have
to call you again? The *Hauptmann* wants to talk to
you."

I climbed slowly up the stone steps.

"Can I help you?" I was shaking. "They've gone
to pray with the other women."

"Come up then, *guaglione*, you'll have to do,"
Donna Livia said.

The *Hauptmann* was sitting in the *salotto* on
Mamma's best chair with one of her pretty little cups
on his lap. "I've been hearing about refugees coming
to town. There's a new employee here, a maid from
someplace, no one knows where." He peered down at

me through his one eyeglass. "Even the mayor seems deficient in information. He doesn't even appear to know who works in his own household. I want to settle this while he's at his meeting. This woman has to present her credentials. What do you know about her?" He set his cup down and glared at me.

"She works for the mayor and *Donna* Livia, sir. She lives here with them, upstairs."

"You are a *Balilla*, aren't you? Loyal to your country?"

"Yes, Sir." I clicked my heels and gave the salute.

"Then tell me. Where is she?"

I looked straight into his cold grey eyes. "I don't know, Sir. The women go to pray every night because of the bombing raids. Women are always fearful."

"You know it is against the law to harbor Jews. Where do they go for this praying you mention?" He dunked his *biscotto* delicately into his coffee and bit off a piece. He didn't drop a single crumb on his uniform.

"I don't know where they are, sir. They gather at the homes of friends. Perhaps they are at church. They didn't tell me."

"You will be a messenger then. When she comes, tell her to bring her papers directly to me. I will hold you responsible. Consider that an ord--"

The sound of a plane flying very low stopped him in the middle of his words, and then there was a huge explosion nearby. The door shook and he knocked the little cup off the table. The *biscotto* went flying. He was off the chair in an instant and out the door. The roar of the motorcycle echoed down the empty street and we heard the sirens start.

"Go back downstairs, then," Livia said. "You're no use to me up here. Just see that you pass that message." She put the tray of cookies back into the cupboard, out of my reach, and clicked the door shut.

Downstairs the fire was almost out in the fire-place. I added some wood and huddled close. I hoped the women didn't find any German officers on their way home. But I waited a long time and they didn't come. Finally, I fell asleep there on the floor.

I woke up stiff and sore. Through the high window I could see the sky getting lighter. There was still no Mamma. No Rosa. I went out and up to the roof bundled up as well as I could. Off to the east the fog was lifting and I could just make out a group walking carefully toward town from the olive fields. Smoke was rising from the place where our field hut was yesterday and a burned patch still glowed on the ground. I'd have to forget about making fireworks out of those discarded explosives.

The women were all wrapped in dark shawls and I could see them picking their way slowly around the big holes that the bombs had made in the road. So they had decided to pray away from town. One, two, three... there were usually at least ten, counting Rosa. These were all the same size, no tall one. No Rosa, sweet and sad and beautiful like Genoveffa in the story at school.

Mamma unlocked the door and let herself in silently. "Get the fire going. Make some noise, drop some wood." She lowered her voice, talked close to my ear. "Don't worry, your lady friend is safe." I could feel my face getting red. "She's in the chapel in the fields. There's a deep closet that few know about. She's cold but she's safe." For the first time I noticed that Mamma didn't have her coat or her sweater, just her shawl, and she was shivering. "We'll prune some olive trees later today. We need firewood anyway. We'll take a big lunch."

In a little bit, Dominic pounded on the door. The sun was hardly up yet. Didn't he ever sleep? "*Ciao.* Have you heard? They're moving out."

"Moving out? Who? How do you know?"

"Come up on your roof..." We ran out and up the stairs. Sure enough, trucks were lining up from the *Campo Sportivo* all along the road, heading north. Soldiers were throwing things into the big *camion* and shouting. In the sports field where the ammo dump had been yesterday, there was a huge hole and men were throwing boxes of papers into the fire. More big trucks were coming toward town from the south and it looked like there were soldiers in them.

"So that's what we heard last night," I said. "No wonder he left so fast. The *Hauptmann* was here and he made me give the *Balilla* pledge. I lied right into his bony face and he believed me."

"You're learning, Peppino. I asked one of them this morning, 'Where are you going in such a hurry?' He said they have new orders," Dominic said. "'New orders,' my tailbone."

"But look at all those *camion* coming towards us." I started to shake. "Maybe they're going to have a big fight right here and we'll all be killed!"

"No. They're on the run. Going to fight

someplace else, and it looks like they won't be coming back. They're packing everything up and burning what they can't take. They wouldn't burn their stuff if they were going to stay. The Allies must be getting close."

We watched them scurry around until Mamma stuck her head out the door and called us in for bread and goat's milk. "We have work to do with those trees today, boys. Eat up, and save some of that bread to take with us. The Germans can take care of themselves."

Later that day while Dominic and I were searching for eggs in the firewood pile, *Donna* Livia came down into the garden in her fur coat. I didn't think she knew how to get there but I kept my mouth shut. "I haven't seen Rosa since she went down to sew last night," she demanded. "Do you think she's taken up with some soldiers? One can't trust servants any more. Have you seen her?"

Mamma narrowed her eyes as she started to speak. But her voice came out level and polite, sweet as fig syrup, so courteous and respectful I could have gagged. "She's gathering fresh firewood for you. The boys will be going shortly with the cart to help her bring it home. She went out early, before full light. You are fortunate to have such a loyal and obedient maid. I could use such help myself, but all I have to help me is this one child, with my husband living far away."

"In America," Livia sneered. "I know what's what around here. People talk. My husband is too soft-hearted, but once the war is over, we'll see who the traitors are." She marched back into the house with her nose in the air.

"Go quickly, boys," Mamma said. "Rosa must be frozen by now. She can ride on the cart coming back, but be sure she gets off and walks once you're in sight of our windows."

Chapter 7
Winter 1943-44

"Do you want to go to the city?" my cousin
Nicola shouted. "We can go to the port and watch
the American ships as they unload. Just see if you
can catch me first." Off he rattled in his two-wheeled
cart pulled by his fast horse. His mother always got
mad at him for racing, but Nicola loved the wind in
his face.

I hitched up my floppy shorts and ran after
him like a maniac over the bumpy stone street. It
was slippery on that December day, and my beat-up
leather shoes slid on the damp stones polished by the
dripping rain. I chased him up one street and down
the other and finally on a tight turn, he slowed down
to avoid an old lady who popped out of her house
chasing her cat with a broom. I grabbed the back
of the wagon and gave a mighty pull to jump up. "I
caught you!" I shouted. "Gotcha!" As I grabbed the

back of the cart my hand slipped on the wet wood and down I went on my elbow. I screamed as the pain shot through me. Nicola yanked his horse to a stop. He jumped off the cart and ran to pick me up.

"You're a fool to chase my horse, *tu sei un vero fesso*," he yelled at me. "Now you've hurt yourself." He wasn't joking and his big brown eyes squinted with worry. My elbow hurt like nothing I had ever felt. He put me gently in the cart and took me home and then the real pain began, when my mother saw that my arm was broken.

"Now what are we going to do? Do you think we can afford a doctor? What are you thinking of, chasing a horse. You're a boy, not a horse." All this discussion didn't make me feel any better.

She went to the chest in front of the hole in the wall and took out a piece of cloth. It had little flowers all over it and looked like it could make a dress. She ripped off some long wide strips and wrapped up my arm firmly. Then she wrapped a long piece like a sash around me so the bone wouldn't move, and sent me to bed.

Nicola apologized and kept out of the reach of her strong arm, escaping with only her voice pounding him. My aunt would be another matter. Now that his chance to get flour from the Red Cross shipment at the harbor was lost, there would be no bread until the next load came in, or until he could steal flour someplace else. My aunt wouldn't be any happier than Mamma.

The next morning Mamma came back from the market really upset, almost crying. "Remember that explosion last night? German planes came back last night and blew up all the ships in the harbor. There's oil and some chemical all over the water. The oil caught on fire."

"But they left last week," I said, shocked. "They piled in their *camion* and drove away."

"They came back with planes," she replied. "The ships were filled with ammunition and fuel and they blew them up. And they say now Bari smells like garlic. All the lights had been on so they could unload supplies. The port was an easy target."

All that excitement and I was stuck in bed with a broken arm. "But didn't the Germans run away?" I asked. "I thought they lost and went up north. I thought they were gone." I couldn't get my mind around it.

"They came back. Never turn your back on an enemy, *figlio mio*. Planes came in low when nobody expected. All along the harbor the windows are blasted out and people are dying everywhere. Michelina saw the fires from her roof. Your Uncle Antonio heard that the people saved from the water are covered with sores. Their skin is hanging off from burns. Some have already died. There's a big fog over everything that is making people sick. "

She hugged me and how my sore arm hurt. "What if you and Nicola were there getting flour for bread? What if the chemicals got to you? What if you got bombed?"

I had never seen her like this before, a new Mamma. I began to think maybe she secretly liked me and just didn't want to let me know.

"What's going to happen Christmas Eve? What about the party?" I asked. "*Nonna* Claudia always

makes a fish party." My mouth started watering just thinking of that party. I really looked forward to the tiny *calamari* with lemon juice squeezed over them. "We're supposed to eat fish and octopus and eels and mussels for Christmas." I was so tired of *pasta e fagioli*.

"Fancy fish! Parties! Don't you use your head, Peppino? There's no party, no fish, no nothing. We're so lucky to have some bread and be still alive!" She stopped hugging and was back to normal. "I'm more worried about poison getting in our *pozzo*, the cistern. Without water to drink and cook with we're in real trouble. American soldiers are going around asking to check people's cisterns for poisons, and if they find it, they seal them up. Let's hope we are far enough away to have clean water."

Soldiers put up roadblocks now and no one could go out or come from the city. There was to be no fishing or fish selling until further notice. The harbor was closed. We heard bits of gossip here and there from people who sneaked through the fields, going around the checkpoints. Everybody going through the *piazza* passed right by *Nonna* Claudia and *Nonno's* house so they heard all the news and passed it on to us.

A few days later I was walking around outside trying not to bump my sore arm. I ran across the barber's son, Nino, in the *piazza*, looking like he'd been dragged behind a wagon. He stumbled along coughing. His shirt and jacket were scorched and stained with oil. His face was pale and his eyes looked yellow around the brown. He kept rubbing them and shaking his head as if he were dizzy. "What happened to you. You're a mess," I said.

"Last Tuesday I went to the city to see if they were starting to bring in the salted fish for Christmas," he said. "I was just hanging around, looking at the American sailors coming off the boats and watching where they go. Restaurants were filling up and there were a lot of shameless girls walking up and down. They were swishing their skirts, and winking at the sailors. I was at the wharf. I wanted to find some sailors to talk to so I could try out my English." He took a deep, shuddering breath.

"All of a sudden, a bunch of planes flew in just above the buildings. They started to drop bombs and shoot. Everybody ran. Ships started blowing up. People were in the water screaming, and there was a disgusting smell of garlic mixed with oil and smoke. Oil and water splashed up and soaked my jacket as I ran along the edge of the wharf. I was lucky I didn't catch on fire."

He stopped and leaned against a wall. He breathed hard for a bit, and then went on. "I just kept running away as fast as I could. The movie theater had a whole wall blown out. You can see the screen from outside. There's a big hole in the cathedral. People lay dead on the street. Americans and British ran around everywhere trying to save their men from the water and bring them to the hospital. I just kept going until I got home." He sat down hard on the stone walk.

"You should go to the doctor. You look really sick."

" I did. Dr. Loconte doesn't know what's wrong with me. He said he's never seen anything like this. He doesn't know of any medicine for it. He says to rest."

"You'll probably be OK," I said. "Probably just got a chill. My mother gives me hot wine and makes me stay in bed. Maybe that would work. Here, lean on my shoulder, no, the other one. I'll help you home."

Two days later Dominic came over. "Did you hear about Nino?"

"Yeah, he caught a chill by the harbor."

"No, he's dead. His skin turned yellow and he kept coughing. He got blisters all over and last night he died. I never heard of a kid dying from a chill..."

When I told Mamma, she cried again. It wasn't like her to cry so often. I started to worry. Maybe the stuff from the harbor killed Nino. We had walked to his house with his oily jacket sleeve around my shoulder. I had my hands on the stuff when I helped him up. How much did it take to make me sick, I wondered. Could I catch whatever he had?

With all the roadblocks we had to rely on gossip to know what was going on. The radio was silent about it. All they announced was that there was to be no fishing or fish selling until further notice. We only learned bits of news from people who sneaked through the fields, going around the checkpoints.

Chapter 8

December 1943

The week before Christmas, *Nonno* knocked softly at our lower door and let himself in. His head drooped and he looked like he was going to cry. "*Sono stato pigliato per fesso, nora mia.* I've been taken for a fool, Daughter-in-law." He pulled a chair near the fireplace and sat down heavily, dropping his cane along side.

"Why? What happened? Don't be so sad." She put her hand on his shoulder.

"Remember that family that asked for refuge right after the attack in Bari? The banker and his wife and the two boys?"

"*Certo.* You took them in. It was very kind, *Papá.* You're a good man, like your son, my Gino. A kind heart. People walk on hearts like yours, though."

"They left this morning, back to Bari. Didn't say good-bye. Didn't say thank you."

"People are nervous and worried, *Papá*. Don't think about it. They want to get back and see if their house is still there."

"That isn't the whole story, Lucia. I carried the sheets downstairs for *Nonna* to wash and things looked different, emptier. Two big rounds of cheese were missing, and a big bottle of the oil we pressed in the fall. A whole sack of flour, too, enough to feed us through the rest of the month. I would have shared some if they asked."

"You're too good, *Papá*. You trust everybody. You think they're all like you. Remember what my own father's partners did when he had a stroke? They sold all his animals and kept the money. He died and we had to scratch to survive."

Nonno hung his head down and shook it slowly. He looked ready to cry. "I know. I'm angry with myself. How could I be so stupid to help strangers and now have my own family without? I thought they just had heavy suitcases. Never dreamed they were full of our winter supplies."

"Another time, *Papá*."

"I know. Don't trust strangers. You don't have to remind me. Lock up supplies. I know better, but I felt sorry for them."

"We'll help," I said. "We can share. I'll get Dominic to keep his eyes open."

"Not by stealing, Peppino. We'll find another way. Maybe we can get supplies next time the Red Cross comes. They'll come soon, now that the road-blocks are gone."

The problem was Christmas. There was nothing to celebrate with. "What is your mother going to make, Dominic?" I asked him. " *Nonno* lost his wheat. Those bums from the city took it. I don't think we're going to have a party at all."

"We can't let that happen. No Christmas? I'll ask my father. He knows some men who—"

"Don't get us in trouble, Dominic. *Nonno* said 'no stealing.' He's too honest—he wouldn't even come to the party if he knew."

"This is the deal. We'll go around to all our cousins and see if they'll each give us just one ration ticket. If we put them all together we can go, you and me by ourselves, to the Red Cross and tell them all our stuff was blown up and maybe they'll give us extra. They feel sorry for kids. Then we can split it up between our families and at least there will be something." So that's what we did.

"Nicola," I told my cousin. "Just get one ticket for us, just one. Your mother won't miss it." And he got us one.

We told the same to every one of my six cousins and Dominic's three aunts and one uncle and his godmother. Even Angelina gave us one and promised not to tell. We got those twelve tickets and took the bus to the city. The harbor still smelled bad, and there were no fishermen selling. Only one stand was open, with salted cod, *baccalá*, from Norway. We got one big piece with two tickets and he gave us a twisted broken one for free. Then on we went to the Red Cross.

Americans were there, unloading a ship. A line had formed, with everyone holding tickets. There was a sign: 1 kilo flour for one ration ticket. We had ten—10 kilos of flour would make a feast. I looked at the line. A woman behind us had three little kids and they were really skinny. The littlest peeked out at us from behind her skirt and his eyes had grey shadows around them.

I tapped Dominic on the shoulder. "What do you think, Dominic?" I said. "We could do this: three for you and three for us and share four?"

"Giving food away? You have a soft heart like your *Nonno* and look what it did for him."

"They're little kids. They didn't cheat anybody. Just two from each of us. It will be their Christmas present."

Dominic nodded slowly and gave a little shrug. He held our place in line while I went to the next four ladies and gave them each one ticket. They couldn't believe it. Their eyes got teary, they were so surprised. I felt like *La Befana*, giving out gifts after Christmas. And it was just a sack of flour—flour for bread, flour to keep them going. Dominic carried our two big sacks most of the way to the bus stop.

As we rode home with our six kilos, Dominic kept looking at me and shaking his head. "You're a crazy, soft kid," he said. "Soft in the head like your *nonno*. Your mother would never do that."

"You'd be surprised," I told him. "She has a heart inside somewhere. She just keeps it under a cover. And besides, this will make a big pile of cookies and we'll eat that fish in tomato sauce so it will make a lot. Christmas in 1943 can be a good one, war or no war."

Chapter 9
January 1944

Even with the Allies pushing the Germans away to the north, it got harder than ever to get bread. We lived on bread—bread for breakfast, bread for lunch if there was any, and bread for supper with some vegetable soup and an egg once in a while. The government issued 100 grams of flour to each person per day. That made one small loaf each to last a whole week. It was brown with lots of stuff in it from the wheat—stems, leaves, sometimes bugs. We didn't like that *pane rustico* much. It gave us a bellyache if it had too many stems. And our Christmas flour was long gone in cookies that we gobbled.

"Why don't you just get some American wheat?" I asked Mamma one day. My mouth watered just thinking about it. "Dominic's father heard it on the radio last night. America sent us a big load of flour to make bread. Maybe it's free."

"Nothing is free, and I know what they're saying, but don't believe it. Your cousin Vito, I know he's not smart, but even Vito has eyes in his head. He went into Bari to try to get some for his family. There was nothing left, just a few sacks with a guard collecting ration tickets for each little bag people filled up. Politicians and their friends got their hands on almost all of it. The only way to get it now is to buy it in *la borsa nera*. No new shipments are coming through the port."

"But *la borsa nera* is against the law, isn't it? We have to turn in tickets to get the food. Anyway where's that market? Can we even find it?"

"We can find it. That's no problem. Just wave some money and it will appear." She looked disgusted. "Maybe just once, to see how it goes, but it's dangerous."

"I'll guard you Mamma. They won't mess with me." She smiled a little. "You're growing up brave, but we have to be careful. Tonight we'll go where Giovan', *il muratore*, told me. He hears a lot as he's fixing damaged houses and he wouldn't put us in danger if he could help it."

That night she took me with her. There was no moon to light our way as we crept along the narrow stone sidewalk. Sounds echoed off the stone streets and houses, so we were careful not to attract the attention of the soldiers enforcing the curfew. She held on to my good arm. After two blocks we spotted a bit of light shining under a door, and she knocked softly.

"*Chi è?*" a voice growled.

"I've come for wheat," Mamma said. "I have

American dollars." The door opened a crack and we went in. Inside there were three strange men there, sitting by a rough table. There were bags of wheat stacked along the side of the room, marked "Red Cross", and a balance scale on the table.

"Why did you bring a kid? Kids talk and talk means trouble," one man grumbled. "If word gets around, we'll all go to jail. The kid will wish he'd never been born."

"No. He won't talk. See, he's stupid, doesn't even hear you. Look, I hit him on the side of the head, he doesn't even fight back." She smacked me, and I bit my lip hard to stifle a cry. "He won't say anything. *Capisce il silenzio.*"

They poured rough grains of wheat into my mother's bag until the scale tipped up even with the weight. I watched, adding up the price. Expensive. Just for wheat. Mamma gave him some paper dollars from before the war that she had hidden inside her dress. I counted as she laid them out. Five times as much as the regular price. Unbelievable.

"Remember, *silenzio,* "the man snarled. He gave me a dirty look and shook his fist in my face. We went home and slowly my heart stopped pounding.

Mamma went to work as soon as we got home. She covered the high window with a dark cloth and got out her hand-cranked coffee grinder. She ground up the rough wheat into flour and made loaves of bread. Once it rose in the morning, the boy from the baker's carried it down the street to bake in the big brick wood-burning oven. Everyone in the neighborhood took turns baking there. I helped her carry it home on a big board, up on my shoulder. My mouth watered all the way.

That first loaf was like bread from heaven, clear white, a bit chewy with a dark crunchy crust you could dunk in oil. When the mayor and his wife were out of sight, I brought up some for Rosa to share. "That's the nicest thing I've tasted since I left Rome," she said. "Bread keeps body and soul together. You can depend on it."

The *borsa nera* stayed in business until the fall when we started to harvest wheat from our own farms. After that the crooks found other things to steal and sell—cars, tires, gasoline, medicine—things we could not grow ourselves.

Chapter 10
February 1944

Ever since Christmas I had been feeling more tired every day.

"You're getting lazy," Mamma finally said. "You're getting *muscia a muscia*, flabby. You never play out with Dominic or your other friends any more. It isn't that cold. We never have snow or ice like *Papá* used to tell about in Chicago."

"I just don't want to go out," I said. "When I try to run, my legs get weak and I have to sit down on the stones. It isn't any fun. I drop the ball all the time. And my arm still hurts all the time."

"Then it's time for *Don* Eduardo to have a look at you. I hope you don't get sick like that barber's boy, Nino. But you didn't go anywhere near the harbor, did you? Did you?!" She peered at me carefully, her dark eyes filled with panic. "Did you go and not tell me? *Eee... Madonna*! If you die, I'll die myself! Here, put on your jacket and tie your scarf tight around your neck. We'll go right now."

The doctor's office was in his house near the church. His wife opened the door when we knocked and led us into the room where he met patients. There was an examining table, two wooden chairs, and a white painted medicine cabinet with glass doors along one green wall. On a shelf on one side stood a steam sterilizer with a row of syringes and needles. He had a strong light in the ceiling, and another that you could shine on the sick person. An old brown table held a microscope and some test tubes in a rack. Above it, the bookshelf was filled with heavy well-thumbed medical books. The whole place smelled of alcohol and soap.

Don Eduardo came in, a stethoscope dangling out of his coat pocket and said, "How can I help you? You're *Signora* Binetti, aren't you the daughter of Sergio Bellino the trader? I don't see you in the *piazza* much any more."

"My husband is away. I don't spend time gossiping in the *piazza*. People would talk."

"Then this young man must be Peppino. I know his grandfather well. What seems to be the problem?" He patted me on the shoulder and I winced. "Something hurting, then? Let's see. Ah, there's a problem with this arm." He took off the flowered wrapping on my arm to have a look—it was still swollen and hurt like mad when he moved it. "This has been broken. How long ago?"

"It was the day of the explosion in Bari," I said before Mamma could reply. "I fell off Nicola's cart."

"That's more than six weeks!" He turned to

Mamma. "Why didn't you bring him then?"

"We can't afford it, *Don* Eduardo. You know with the war there is no money in the mail from America and the Germans have been taking so much of the food—"

"Healing comes first, money comes second. You should know that of me, *Signora*. People pay when and if they can. I would have taken care of him." He felt the arm all over, up and down, pressing firmly all along. He shook his head and pressed his lips together. "Now it's too late to make any changes in the arm. I'd have to break it again to make it straight. I'll just give him a new wrapping. One with no flowers. As he grows the curve may straighten out."

He smiled at me. "Big boys like you don't want flowered bandages. Let me see if I have one a soldier could be proud of." He turned his back and went to dig around in a cabinet. "Here's one," he said, pulling out a roll of white strips that looked like they were once sheets. He lifted my arm gently. "Crooked arms still do the job. Why did you come now?"

"He's getting weak and tired all the time. He doesn't want to play," Mamma said. "He's not as lively as he was."

While she talked, he was looking into my eyes, pulling down the lid to see the lining. He pinched the ends of my fingers and looked at the color of my fingernails. He looked in my mouth and down my throat. Lifted up my shirt and listened to my heart. He didn't let her talking stop him from his work.

"I want to do a blood test, *Signora*. It will probably give us the answers."

"Do you think he's sick like the barber's son, Nino, Doctor? The one who died?"

"That was a strange case, never saw anything like it. It almost seemed as if he'd been poisoned. His body simply quit making proper blood cells and he was gone before we knew it. A tragedy..." He turned to me. "You weren't near the harbor that day, were you?"

"No, that's the day I broke my arm. I was on my way there with my cousin. I talked to Nino, though, after. I helped him walk home. I touched his oily jacket."

"I don't think that did you any damage, my boy. Poison doesn't spread like a cough or measles. Let's have a look at that blood of yours."

I wasn't happy to hear that. I'd already seen the big syringes and needles up on the shelf. Sure enough, he rolled up the sleeve on my good arm and wrapped a piece of rubber tube tightly around above my elbow. He put alcohol on a piece of cotton and wiped my arm. Then he went to the sterilizer and fished a clean syringe and needle out with a tongs. He slipped the needle into my arm and took out some blood. It looked like a lot but on the syringe it said 5 cc., only about a spoonful. He loosened the tubing and held the cotton tight against my vein.

"Here, *Signora*, hold this tight. Don't make him use his sore arm."

He went to his microscope table and put a drop of that blood into a tiny glass tube, added some liquid, shook it and put a drop onto a glass plate to use under the microscope.

"Come have a look, Peppino. See. Look at the

plate. It's divided up into very tiny squares so we can count your blood cells."

I looked in. I could see little pink things like life preservers floating and tumbling on a grid.

"Once they settle, I can count them and multiply and figure out how many blood cells you have. If you don't have enough, we call it anemia and that would explain why you're tired all the time. There may not be enough blood to carry your food and oxygen around."

Amazing, I thought. Just a drop of blood and some math. I wish I could do stuff like that. That would be a job worth doing.

After a couple of minutes he looked into the microscope and started counting, wrote down the answer, did some multiplying and said," Yes, it's anemia all right. He is lacking about 1/5 of the blood cells he needs. Does he eat much meat?"

"Meat? In a war? You're joking, *Dottore*. Sometimes we kill a rabbit, if we have one. At Christmas we shared a chicken with eight people."

"Nevertheless, *Signora*, meat is what he needs. Not just any meat. He needs to eat liver and spleen. I'll write out a prescription so you can get extra ration tickets for him. Then go every week, twice if you can, and get a piece of liver or spleen at the butcher shop. They'll roast it on their big grill and he can eat it right there. That's the cure. Feed him lamb spleen or lamb liver twice a week until he feels strong again. And don't worry about my fee. When you get some nice vegetables in your garden, you can send this strong boy over with a bag of them. That's all I want." He patted me on the shoulder and left the room.

Going home, I asked Mamma "Is he that nice to everybody?"

"*Nonno* says he's a saint," she replied. "Once during the bombing, a woman was having a baby and it got stuck and couldn't come out. He took her in his car to the *Policlinico* in Bari so she could be saved. Drove right up the road with bombs falling all around. They were able to operate there and she lived. So did the baby. He's a good man, what a doctor should be."

On the way home we stopped at the *municipio* and got the ration tickets, and then at the butcher for the lamb. They gave me a slice, all roasted and rolled up in a cone of brown paper so I could eat it like an ice cream cone. It was good and warm and the juice ran down my chin. I gave Mamma a bite, too, but she made me eat the rest so I'd get strong.

Chapter 11
Early Spring 1944

Right after the Germans moved out, the British soldiers had started coming in. "What happened to the Americans?" I asked Mamma. She didn't know. I asked Dominic and he didn't either. Neither did Angelina. She was my last choice because she chewed on garlic for her health and I wanted to keep my nose out of her range. Finally I worked up the nerve to go to Z'Antonio's office and ask his secretary if I could talk to him.

"Your uncle is very busy right now sorting out the paperwork for the land around here," she said. "Different armies have taken over people's houses, and fields are destroyed so some families are arguing over who owns what. It's a total mess."

"I only have a quick question," I said. "He has the only radio in town. Maybe he knows what's really true."

"What's going on out there?" called a voice from the inner office. "Work is piling up—there's no time for gossip."

"It's your nephew, Peppino. Shall I send him in?"

"I guess I have time for my brother's boy. Come in, Peppino."

"Hi, *Z' Tonino*. I just need to know. What happened to the Americans? They were going to come and save us. Now the place is full of British soldiers. They look up words in small books and they're hard to talk to. Where are the Americans?"

"On the news last night they said the Allied armies divided up the job. The English are coming up along this side near the Adriatic, and the Americans plan to come across after they conquer Naples and Sicily." He leaned forward in his chair, ran his hands through his hair and sighed. " They must have run into trouble or they'd already be here. You know Italy made peace with them, but now there's no trust. Almost everyone is mad at the Italians and we're mad at each other, too. Tell your Mamma that the best plan is to keep quiet, hang on to your food and try not to get shot by anyone!"

Well, now at least I knew something. The Americans hadn't quit after all. They were just delayed. I just knew they wouldn't quit on us.

I found Dominic near the *piazza* kicking his ball, practicing serves against a wall. "Want to play, Peppino? Just look how I can put spin on it. I'll see if I can hit that guy going into the *municipio*, the guy in short pants. Doesn't he know it's still winter?"

"He's a soldier, Dominic, even with shorts.

The British may wear short pants but they're tough. They chased the Germans out, didn't they?"

"I don't care. Just watch. Here goes!" Dominic hauled off and kicked that ball so hard, turning his foot a little as he did to give it some spin. It sailed up and across and took the officer's hat right off his head. He was surprised, but we were dumbfounded. His hair popped up and it was bright flaming orange. Bright orange, not furniture-polish red like the mayor's wife had. He looked like he had a fire on his head, standing there holding a box of papers with a puzzled look on his face. I didn't think he could shoot us with his arms full of papers but I started to run just to be on the safe side.

"Hullo there, boys. You'll be needing that ball. Heads up!" With that he gave the ball a mighty kick that sent it back almost to the row of palm trees by the park.

We couldn't believe it. One of the German army would've shot us for sure, or at least yelled. This one was a different sort.

"We'd better apologize," I told Dominic.

We went over. "*Scusate signor ufficiale*," we said. Sure enough, he pulled a little book out of his pocket. "*Scusate*... let me see. That would be under "s"—s,c,oo—no, scu..." He was having a hard time. This could take all afternoon.

"Talk *Inglese*," we said. "We learn American. Say again. My name Peppino."

"My name Dominic."

"All right then, I'll have a go... My name Reggie Thorton, Staff Sergeant, British 5th Army. Rugby player."

"Rugby. *Cos 'è?* What it is, Rugby?"

"It's a game. We chase the ball and fight over it and kick it. We don't kick it at people's heads though." He gestured to his head as if he was knocking his hat off and shook his head "No."

"Won't do any more, not you. You not shoot us."

"Did you expect to get shot? Then why do it?"

"I thought, maybe," Dominic said. "I run fast, before gun." He pointed at the soldier's pistol.

"I'm done with shooting at present," Thorton said. "Now I'm a desk jockey here, sorting papers and permits for this town to try to get it in order. We're setting up an office here for ration cards and such. I've seen all the shooting I want to see for the rest of my life. Now I'm a desk man. Come 'round or send your mum if you need anything."

We understood "ration," "desk," and "Mum" because it sounded like mamma. We tried to say Thorton, but all those "h's" were impossible.

"Can we call you nickname?" Dominic said. "Friend name? Easy to say?"

"What do you have in mind?"

"You'll be *Capu' russ'*, red head. We be friends then. That's what friends do."

He opened his little book again. "Cap...? Here it is. It's *Ca-po*. That's head. Now *rosso*...red. Red head."

"*Si. Si.* I said. *Capu' russ'*. Means same."

"Very well. I'll be Staff Sergeant 'Red-head' if it pleases you. No skin off me. Now be off with you. I have some heavy paper-pushing to do."

Chapter 12
March 1944

It was almost the end of Lent. There weren't any treats to give up, so we said extra prayers. Mamma made me go to church Friday and Sunday. The lamb in the basement was growing bigger every day and soon I knew *Nonno* would kill it with a quick cut for our Easter dinner. Mamma had been saving ration coupons and serving *rapini* and beans for almost four weeks. Those coupons would get us good flour to make sweet bread, and we could have *taralle* for dessert. The almond trees were blooming and smelled wonderful, with little pink flowers all over the full field. The port of Bari was open now and a few fishermen were daring enough to fish, steering carefully between the mines as they went. Things were looking up.

One morning when I woke up, everything was covered with dark gray dust, like snow, only blackish. It was 3-4 cm thick, and piled in little drifts in corners like the snow in pictures *Papá* sent before the war. I ran out to the garden. Every plant was covered in gray. All the orange and lemon flowers on our trees were dusted, and the little salad plants that were starting to grow were covered, too. And it was still falling from the sky like black snow, drifting down steadily and coating the world with gray. I started to cough as I came back into the house.

"Mamma, what's all that stuff outside? The whole world looks dirty."

"It looks like ashes to me, Peppino. Maybe that volcano near Naples... but that's too far away. Go see what you can find out, but cover your nose and mouth with your scarf in case it really is ashes. They'll get into your lungs and make you sick."

I dressed fast and wrapped my scarf over my nose and mouth. I didn't like the wool. It tasted like smoke and barn and it made my nose itch. Out I went into the gray world. Every step I took stirred up clouds of that gritty dust that crunched on the stones underfoot. I noticed off to the west that the sky was pretty dark, too dark for mid-morning. Sergeant Thorton was crossing the street. "Hey, *Capu' russ'*," I called. "I want ask you—"

"If it isn't my little friend the soccer player. How's it going, Peppino?"

"OK, getting ready for Easter. But what's wrong with sky?" I pointed west. "Dark should start east. Today dark in west and getting windy. Gray stuff is like black snow. Is bombing? Or fire?"

"Ah, must be the volcano. Did you hear? The volcano erupted near Naples. Vesuvio, it's called.

Poured lots of melted lava down the sides over a number of houses, and today the army reported a fiery explosion and a big ash cloud moving this way. Don't expect the planes will be going anywhere for a bit. That ash has pumice dust in it and it jams the propellers."

"You mean more is coming here? Will it burn us up?"

"No, just a lot of gritty dust, I expect. Advise your mum not to put out washing."

As I kept going toward Dominic's place, it kept getting darker. Soon the wind was blowing the black powder over everything. It got in my eyes. It was hard to breathe through the scarf and it kept slipping down. I gave up on playing with Dominic and headed home. By the time I got there everything was covered deeper. "Help me block these cracks," Mamma said. "That dust is getting to everything." I helped her stuff rags in the bigger cracks. There was a big crack under the *portone* door and we piled sacks against it. Still the dust filtered in, making us cough. Our eyes were sore even inside. The thin layer on top of the table felt sandy, gritty and I could hear my shoes scratch against the stone floor as I walked.

Late in the afternoon the city sent out workers to clean up, so the streets looked better. The plants still looked grimy, though. *Nonno* came with two big buckets. "Here, help me sweep up as much as we can for fertilizer," he said. "It's dirty for us, but it feeds the plants." We worked together with our faces covered like bandits and filled up about four buckets. He spread it around on the dirt under our tomato plants, and took a couple of buckets home to add to his own. The farmers were happy to have that free fertilizer from the sky on their fields.

That was a good year for olives and almonds. You could smell the sweet flowers in the fields, the tiny white ones on the olive trees and the pink clouds of almond blossoms. If every flower made a fruit, we'd have a good crop this year, enough to eat and plenty to sell.

Chapter 13
Late Summer 1944

In August in the little park near the *piazza*, Dominic spotted three American GI's eating lunch around their jeep. We knew they were Americans because they wore jeans and sailor hats. No shorts for the Americans. They had found a park bench under some palm trees and had made themselves comfortable.

"Let's get some lunch, Peppino. I dare you."

"That's stealing, Dominic. We'll get in trouble."

"What are you, a girl? 'We'll get in trouble.' What a baby. I thought you were the man of the family."

That really hit me. "I am not a girl!" I swung at him and missed. He laughed. "I run around, see, and get them to look at me, and you just grab the food. Then run like hell."

Dominic headed around the jeep, making faces and laughing. He wasn't fast enough. A big GI with arms like a wrestler grabbed him and held him with his face against the jeep.

Another one, tall and skinny, wearing denim pants and glasses, came over and said, in very strange Italian, *"Puoi chiedere com' un gentiluomo.* You can ask like a gentleman."

I was so surprised to hear Italian of any kind coming out of the American's mouth. I stood up straight like we do in school, clicked my heels like a good *Balilla*, saluted and politely asked, *"Posso avere qualche cibo americano?* May I have some American food?"

The tall sailor laughed and so did the others. Dominic was still wiggling and trying to kick the big one who held him, but he was no match for him. The sailor had big muscles like Popeye in the cartoons and a tattoo of an anchor on his arm, too. The GI's looked at us and then at each other.

"Check their knees, Joe. He's pretty pale for a kid in summer in Italy," Popeye said, "and skinny, too."

"Do you want to try some meat? *Volete carne?"* Joe gave me a piece of pink meat from a can. He offered one to Dominic if he would hold still. Dominic opened his mouth like a baby bird.

That was the most amazing food I ever had. It was pink and looked like sausage, but I couldn't tell what it was made of. Not lamb, not rabbit, not chicken… and it was sort of square and soft, but not too soft. It smelled like sausage, or maybe ham—a little salty. Something completely new.

"*Cos' è?* What is it?" we wanted to know.

"It's called Spam and the Navy feeds it to us every day."

"Meat every day?" Now, that was unbelievable. No wonder they could fight, with their bellies full of meat.

"What's your name, kid? *Come ti chiami?* I'm Joe Governale, U.S. Merchant Marine." He gave a little salute and pushed his glasses up higher on his nose.

"*Mi chiamo Binetti Giuseppe, ma tutti mi chiamano Peppino.* My name is Giuseppe Binetti but everybody calls me Peppino."

"OK, Peppino. Now, we can give one can to each of you to take home. One for you and one for your friend *il ladro* here, the thief."

"He's Dominic."

"OK. Dominic. *Vieni qui.* See how we open it." He found a twisted wire thing on the can, broke it off and poked a strip at the top of the can through the slot. He turned the wire around and around like a key and that metal strip just peeled right off. It looked like a gooey spring and when he was done the can opened and there was a whole big piece of that pink Spam meat ready to eat.

"*Signor* Joe, why you talk Italian? You're American."

" My mom and dad are from Italy, but we live in New Jersey. My mom came from Calabria when she was a baby and my dad is Sicilian." His Italian was slow, one word at a time like my English.

So that's why he talks so funny, I thought. His languages are all mixed up.

"How can you all talk to each other?"

"Well, they must have. I have two little sisters," he laughed. "Take this home to your parents."

I ran home with my can of Spam clutched to my chest. What a crazy country, America, I thought. People from all over are making families when they can hardly talk. Sending their sons to other places to fight and then they give away perfectly good food. *Pazzi*," I said to myself, *sono tutti pazzi*.

I found Mamma hanging up my other shirt on the roof to dry. "I have meat, Mamma, meat from the Americans."

"So, now you're taking food from strangers? What have I told you? It could be poisoned!" She put her hands on her hips and frowned at me.

"No, Mamma. They're GI's. That's what they call the Americans. Dominic was trying to steal their lunch, and they caught him, and they gave us some meat to taste, and it's good, and they let us go." I could hardly get the words out fast enough.

"They're strangers, *forestieri!* We don't know them or their families or where they're from. Besides, we're not beggars. We own land and we work for what we have."

"You have to listen to me, Mamma. Joe is from New Jersey in America. His mom is Calabrese and his dad is Sicilian. He told me all about his family. He has two sisters. He talks Italian funny but I can understand him. He says I talk funny, too."

"New Jersey? Your *papá* has a cousin who married a woman from New Jersey. And he talked to you and Dominic? With respect? They didn't touch you or hurt you?"

"They were good, Mamma. They thought it was funny that Dominic tried to steal their food. They gave us each some meat. They call it Spam and they eat it every day and they don't like it much because they have so much of it."

She broke off a little piece and tasted it. "Pretty good. Not my own sausage, but a big improvement over beans," she said. "You say they have too much of it? They're tired of it? I should be so rich to get tired of meat every day. Still we don't want to be under obligation to these people. We'll get a sack of tomatoes and you can run right back and give them to the soldiers, *per disobbligare*." She got about 10 ripe tomatoes off our vines, and some salad, and put them in a cloth shopping bag. "*Vai! Vai! Port' indietro il sacco*, bring back the bag. And don't stay around there."

As I ran back to the park, I saw them getting into the jeep to go. The blond guy I called Popeye shouted, "Hey, Governale, your little friend is back and wants to see you. You're just a regular Pied Piper, aren't you?" The fatter one with a wrinkled sailor cap said "Now, if you could only work your magic on some girls." Joe turned to me, looking surprised. "Mamma give tomatoes," I said. "*Per disobbligare. Nonno* has garden."

"What else do you grow?"

All of a sudden, I got scared. What if they came and took all our vegetables, like the Germans used to take the eggs and sheep? Me and my big mouth. Would I never learn to be *furbo*?

" I can't tell. It's our own food, we grow it to

eat. There's not much. It's not very good. Wall with glass pieces on top." I was really mumbling by now, more scared of Mamma than the sailors. She'd never forgive me if they robbed us.

Joe said, "Look, we have a lot of this spam and all our food comes in cans. What if we trade? You get things you like and we get some fresh vegetables."

"Maybe I can sell. *Quanto costa* four Spam?" I held up four fingers and pointed.

"What can you give us? What do you have?" Now I knew he was Sicilian, making deals.

"One bag, one can." I pointed to my bag and a tin, so he could understand. "And one American dollar," I added, pointing to along the street and then my feet.

"Shipping? This kid's a riot! He's shipping his stuff all of half a mile," Art, the fatter one, said. "Not like us, shipping oil and ammo across the ocean, hospital supplies, too."

"Shoes, old, stones on street. Not help at home. *È basta!* That's the deal."

"OK," Joe shook my hand. "We come back into port every three weeks. Come here three weeks from today, Monday afternoon, and we'll do business."

So I went into the vegetable business. They bought a lot from *Nonno*, too, all the tomatoes we could spare, lots of salad, green beans, some late figs, peppers. Dominic traded some eggs. As it got cooler, we had lemons and oranges from *Nonno*'s walled-in trees to sell. *Capu' russ'* told the British officers at the *municipio*, and my business grew. We traded for other things besides Spam— toothpaste, shoelaces, iodine to put on cuts, aspirin, a couple of pairs of very big socks...useful things. And I got a dollar every time on the side that I hid in a crack in the basement wall.

It used to be more exciting to steal the shoe-laces from the Germans, more fun than garden selling. Shoelaces were boys' business. If soldiers left their shoes outside to dry out, we'd nip the shoelaces out and then sell them at the market. The Germans had gone through lots of shoelaces that way, especially when they sent them to the shoemaker. Shoes always came back to them without laces. They got "lost" during the fixing. Managers in Germany probably wondered why the soldiers in Italy needed so many shoelaces. The British took better care of their stuff, so I got out of that business.

Stealing wasn't a very good business, though. One time another friend called *Mincuccio U'Surd,* because his left ear didn't work, was eating grapes in his grandpa's field. Saverio, the *guardia campestre* who patrolled the fields, spotted him. Saverio was mean, the kind of person who thinks he runs the world because of his badge. If he caught a child, he'd really beat him up all black and blue. One day *Nonna* Claudia had seen him march two men all across town carrying bunches of grapes that they'd stolen because they were hungry. He wanted to embarrass them in front of everybody.

Well, Saverio spotted Mincuccio and started to chase him with his club. Mincuccio was a little guy and fast on his feet. He took off between the vines with the cop at his heels. Up one row and down the other they went. It was touch and go until Saverio's big belly wore him out and he had to sit down.

Mincuccio just danced around out of reach, calling
him names and making rude gestures. He had a great
collection of nasty ones.

Cigarettes were good business, too, because
the soldiers used to throw their used cigarette butts
away. Some tobacco was always left. We boys walked
around in the *piazza* looking casual, and the first kid
who spotted one would snatch it up and put it in his
pocket. Kids had good eyes, not worn out from studying. Schools were still closed. We'd go in somebody's
shed and ravel out the tobacco to make new cigarettes to sell. Tobacco was almost impossible to buy
in a store.

Chapter 14
Late Fall 1944

More and more British and American soldiers started coming into our town that fall. A few in a jeep would drive in and look around, talk to some of us. A couple Americans tried to talk Italian but it was pitiful to hear. Their families must have come from a different Italy.

"Outsiders!" Mamma said. "*Forestieri!* Don't trust them. Don't tell them anything. Don't take anything from them. We don't know their families. They may not all be nice like Joe. Who knows what they're up to?"

"They're Americans, Mamma, like where *Papá* lives. They're good. They're going to save us."

"Nobody saves anybody unless they're getting something out of it. Stay away, I tell you!"

But of course all of us boys wanted to talk to them. They drove cars, carried guns. They were tough, and they had chased out the Germans who stole our food. They looked like heroes to us. They talked to us, called us 'kids.'

"Chew gum, kid?" they'd say.

"Choo-choo gomma," we'd say back, thinking we were learning to talk American. Then they'd give us this stuff they called gum. It was delicious, sweet, sticky and pink. I swallowed the first piece I got and asked for more.

"You don't eat it. You chew it all afternoon. It will make you forget you are hungry," they said. We chewed and chewed and somebody discovered that you could pull it out of your mouth and stretch it almost as long as your arm, then put it back. Amazing.

The GI's gave us other good stuff, too, sometimes an old army hat, or some well-worn socks. Dominic even got some boots, way too big and all beat up. He stuffed the toes and wore them around in the *piazza* showing off. What he really wanted was a German pistol, but none of them would give one up.

GI's threw away longer cigarette butts than the British did, so we found lots to collect. That was like money found on the street. Some of them talked to the big girls too, and one gave Angelina's daughter Paolina some thin nylon stockings. When I told Mamma she spit on the ground and called her a bad word. If I had a sister I think Mamma would have locked her in the basement.

"*Signor* Cataldo got a movie," Dominic said one Friday afternoon. "Maybe we can sneak in the back and watch from the balcony. It's a cowboy one with Tom Mix."

Cataldo used to put a big white cloth screen up at the front of a room and sell tickets for 25 *lire* to anyone who wanted to come. Nobody's mother would give any *lire* or money at all, so we couldn't go. I wasn't going to waste my cigarette money on a movie. But sneaking in the back door that was left open for air, that sounded good.

"I'll go," I said. "You first. I'll talk to him and get him to look away. Then once you're in, I'll wait around and come up." The heroes always won in those movies—bang, bang and the bad guys were gone. After we got our system working, we did it every Friday.

We loved to see Laurel and Hardy. I giggled when Oliver would say, "A fine mess you got us into this time, Stanley!" when he made stupid mistakes. Even with all the mistakes, he always came out ahead. I used to say it to Dominic, "Fine mess, you got us into this time, Stanley!" and we'd get a good laugh.

"I wish I could go on one of those boats out across the sea," I told Dominic one time. "Like in *C'era una volta un' piccolo naviglio*, Once There Was a Little Boat. I could just sail away with some funny guys and get out of here."

"That's a dumb idea," Dominic said. "You're stuck here just like me. We're planted like old trees and we'll never move. Our families won't let go of us."

"Maybe," I told him. "Just maybe."

Sometimes the rented movies were too long, and *Signor* Cataldo would cut pieces out of the film and glue the ends back together. He threw the cut out parts out back with the trash. We used to glue those pieces into a new movie. We'd hold them up to a light in somebody's basement and see movies of our own.

The soccer field was all torn up by the military camp, so we'd find an empty part of the *piazza*, put a rock to mark each corner and play. There were no grownups, and we made our own rules. We didn't worry about a few bruises from the stones on the street.

One time our homemade ball finally fell apart. On a shopping trip to Bari for some cloth, I spotted one. "Will you buy me a ball, Mamma? Our ball is all in pieces. Please?" I asked in my nicest sweet voice.

"You want a ball? A toy? Do you think we're rich? Do you see gold in my house? Do we have a car? Even a horse? A bicycle? Keep your mind on important things!"

I pestered and argued, and finally when all else failed, I cried. But she was made of sterner stuff. Nothing worked. I cried all the way home on the bus, sniffing and slurping and looking out of the side of my eyes to see if she was softening up. People told her, "Buy him the blasted ball for heaven's sake." One lady offered to buy the ball herself, just to shut me up.

"Mind your own business," Mamma replied sharply. When she made up her mind, it stayed made up.

Chapter 15

Spring 1945

"Mamma, what do you think of Mussolini? Is he good or bad?" I asked one morning. "I heard some men sitting outside their club yesterday and they were yelling at each other about it. Nobody was hitting, but they were really mad at each other. Mimmo's uncle kept shouting and pounding on the table. One of the British MP's came over and told them to settle down."

"Mussolini was good at first, working for the King. He gave all the kids free school until 4th grade. He built the *acquedotto* with pipes to bring in clean water from the mountains to the fountains. But power went to his head. He got gangs called Black Shirts to beat up the opposition. They'd come around and ask which party you were voting for, and then beat you up or set fire to your house if they didn't agree. It was too bad he ever met Hitler. That messed up his head. He forgot how to tell right from wrong."

"What do you mean? How could he not know?"

"He started thinking Italy could be a world ruler. Wanted to be like Julius Caesar. He sent the army to take over places in Africa—Libya, Ethiopia—as if we needed more hot deserts. Then he declared war on America. What a dumb thing to do. It got us in so much trouble. America isn't something to mess with."

"I thought we liked America. So many fathers live there already." I was puzzled.

"Right. They do. So now Italy has made peace with America and Germany is getting even with us. Italians are fighting each other and not just outside the bar. The government changes from week to week.   Italians quit our own army in disgust and just walk home. You know Uncle Carlo just walked home more than hundred miles with his uniform shirt hidden under a stolen jacket. Now the King has put Mussolini in jail in the north and the Germans want to save him. It's a mixed-up *pasticcio*, and the people always suffer."

"Can people be that stupid, Ma'? There has to be more to it. A whole country changing sides?"

"Never underestimate how stupid people can be, Peppino. Especially when they smell power."

I went to see what *Capu' russ'* thought and check with Joe. I wanted to hear all the facts. "What about Mussolini?" I asked the Sergeant.

"He's a bloody tyrant, not to put a fine point on it," he said. "Dragging his country after him to follow that criminal Hitler, and now leaving his people between a rock and a hard place."

"What about rocks? I not understand."

"It's a way of speaking. I mean he's left them between two fighting armies. No way to win."

"What's going to happen?"

"The Allies are winning more every day, moving north. The Americans have liberated Naples and Rome. The Americans hold the airfields near here around Foggia. We have the Port of Bari to bring in supplies."

" I know. Have friends work on ships—Joe, Art, Popeye— all those."

"The Germans are in trouble but they're trying to hang on north of Pescara. They raided the jail and got Mussolini out yesterday."

"He's out? Will he come back? Then the Germans come back, too? " I was worried. We didn't want them coming back. Just then his assistant came running out of the office, all excited. "Look at this, Sergeant Thorton. A cable just came in. Mussolini has been caught by the *partigiani* and they've killed him. Just grabbed him from the Germans, they did. Him and his lady friend. He's finished. That's the end of the bloody bastard. Begging your pardon, Sergeant."

"That seems to have settled his hash, then, my boy. You have an answer to your questions. This will give a lot of encouragement to the Allies I expect. And it serves him bloody right. Turning his country this way and that and leaving them to be bombed by both sides." Just then I saw the Vituccio the *banditore* coming across the *piazza*. He was shouting "*È morto Mussolini! È stato ucciso!* Mussolini is dead!

He's been killed!"

As I ran back to tell Mamma, people were spilling out of all the houses to talk about it, as the news raced through town. Even with only one radio and six telephones, news spread like a fire in a hay field. By the time I got home, the news had already reached Mamma. "That will show him," she said. "Causing us all this trouble. *Maledetto demonio!* Cursed devil!" This was her real opinion, now that it was safe to say it out loud.

The next morning when I woke up I didn't hear the water in the pipes. It was strange not to hear any walking or yelling. Usually *Donna* Livia would be giving loud orders to Rosa by now, or banging a skillet on the stove. I went out the small door and climbed up to the roof. Nobody was there. Back downstairs I told Mamma.

"Maybe they're sleeping late. Don't bother them. You know how *Donna* Livia is when she's tired."

By noon, though, she was curious, too. We hadn't heard a sound. We went around to our own front door and knocked. No answer. We knocked again. Still no answer. After the third knock, we heard Rosa whispering near the keyhole. "Who is it? The mayor is not at home."

"It's us. Lucia and Peppino. Why are you whispering? Are they still sleeping?"

She opened the door, grabbed Mamma in a big hug, and pulled us inside. "They're gone," she said. "When it got dark, they packed up all their clothes and personal things in suitcases. They got their money out of the little safe and put it with her jewelry

in a sack that Livia tied around her waist. They made
one phone call, and then crept outside. A big dark car
came and picked them up and they drove off. Didn't
say anything. I watched behind the kitchen door.
They didn't even say good-bye."

"Another rat leaves the ship," Mamma said.
"It's a sign, Peppino. Americans are moving north,
British are running things in Bari, Mussolini is dead,
and now this Fascist bag of dirt sneaked out. Big
changes are happening. Things will be better from
now on. Once we're sure they're not coming back,
we'll move back into our house. We'll take baths as
often as we like and pee in a toilet and wash dishes
under a faucet. Thanks to God, we'll have our house
back."

That night we went upstairs and looked
around. The furniture was all there. The table
was scuffed and there was a little rip in one of the
chair cushions, as if it had snagged on something.
Mamma counted the china and it was all there in
the glass-fronted cabinet, all except the cup that the
Hauptmann dropped when the ammunition dump
blew up. Otherwise, it looked like home. A pile of
ashes was in the sink where papers had been burned,
and all their pictures had been taken off the walls.
You could smell *Donna* Livia's perfume in the big
bedroom. The house was empty and ours again.

"I wonder where I should go now," Rosa said
to Mamma the next day as we were carrying the table
upstairs.

"You have no home at all? No family?"

"No. I was alone even in Rome because my
parents died young. You know my fiancé Primo

hasn't been heard of since the Nazi raid. As soon as the Americans took over Rome, I wrote to my old boss. After three months he wrote back, through *Don* Silvestro. He said Rome was still in turmoil and none of those who were shipped away last year had been seen again. There was a rumor that they were all sent to Auschwitz and killed. Probably Primo was among them. I have no one at all. I'm not sure if Borgati is even in business now."

"Oh, no, Rosa. Everyone needs to belong to someone. Do you want to stay here with us? You can help me and I can help you. When things get better you can think of something else, but for now just stay with us."

"Oh, Lucia. How kind. I won't let you down."

"Why don't you stay in the front bedroom? Peppino can sleep in my room. You shouldn't be sleeping on a kitchen floor like a dog."

So that's what we did. I lost my room, but I didn't mind. I liked Rosa. We moved up into the main house and it all seemed new after living downstairs.

The best thing was the bathroom. Big shiny tiles covered the walls, and there was a tub with a faucet and a pipe on top that would sprinkle water down on me. A water tank on the wall had a gas burner inside that I could light if I wanted my bath to be warm. The toilet had another tank above it to let water down and flush. The sink had two faucets and we could get cold water from either one. Standing on the toilet I could look through the window high up on the side of the house, to see what was happening on the pharmacist's roof. Not much happened there, mostly drying tomatoes and laundry. Sometimes the pharmacist's wife came out and sat in a wooden chair letting the warm spring sun warm her face. She'd roll her black stockings down to let the heat soak into her sore knees and just sit there alone, looking content.

The kitchen made Mamma so happy. She almost forgave the mayor. There was a water faucet over the sink and a drain underneath to carry the dirty water away. No more *pozzo*, no more buckets, no more pots for bathrooms. We were living in style. Giovan' came back and dug the good pots out of the wall. Mamma put her dishes back in the cabinet. Our clothes went back into the *armadio*. I dug my vegetable business money out of the crack in the basement wall and put it between the sofa cushions. Life was worth living. We were happy again.

Chapter 16
May 8, 1945

The bells woke me up from my nap. First the big bells in the main church started and then all the little churches and chapels joined in. Low bongs, high ones—every church sounded different. They kept ringing and ringing and not letting up. "What's going on?" I yelled. "Are the bombers coming back? Should we hide?" All my life ringing bells meant danger. Yet something was different.

Mamma seemed happy. I found her in the kitchen making *orzo* coffee out of roasted barley, smiling and humming to herself, not serious as she usually was. She gave me a big hug. Rosa was singing to herself as she toasted pieces of bread on a long fork over the flame on the stove. "No. This time it's good news. The war is over. They signed a peace agreement last night and the war in Europe is officially done. The Germans have given up, Hitler is dead and life can go on. *Z'Antonio* came over to tell me as soon as he heard it on the radio."

Wow, I thought. I took a nap and the whole world changed when I wasn't looking. I ran up to the roof to see. People were coming out of all the houses and hugging each other. Some put flags out of their windows, Italian and some American too. A group passed by singing a hymn and heading for the church. I heard Vituccio *U'Ca Caat,* his voice too big for him, marching along in his baggy pants, shouting from the end of the street. *"La guerra è finita!* The war is over!" he shouted over and over. *"La guerra è finita!"* His voice rang against the limestone houses and hard granite cobblestones. A dead person couldn't sleep with all the noise. People brought out pots and started banging them. I could see that Mussolini didn't get them all.

On the corner close to the *piazza* I heard the band tuning up. Somebody must have gone to wake them up right away because here they were, while everyone else was still napping, starting to play. They played *Va Pensiero,* the song everyone knew from the opera about the Jewish slaves longing for their homeland. They played marches from Sousa and then started on the hymns. People sang along. It was a big party. Women were crying and laughing. Mamma and Rosa found their friends and everybody hugged everybody. Men slapped each other on the back and hugged. People brought out wine and served it to anyone who passed by. I spotted Sgt. Thorton and his team coming in toward their office in the jeep, throwing paper scraps like confetti and looking like they already had quite a lot of wine. Everybody talked at once.

Now we can go to America, I thought. We can pack up and get out of here. Go to a new life. I told that to Dominic when I found him.

"Don't get your hopes up," he said. "It costs a lot of money and you have a farm and business here. Your family won't let you get away."

"Maybe *Papá* will come here then. Somehow we can get this family back together. You'll see."

"*Speriamo*," he replied. "Let's hope."

The feast in Conversano was coming up the next week. Every town has its own feast for its special saint. A lot of them are for the Blessed Virgin, but under different names. Conversano's big feast was for *Madonna della Fonte*, Our Lady of the Fountain, no one knows why. There was probably an old story behind it. But this year there was a lot to celebrate. This was going to be the best feast in a long, long time.

We went there early on the bus and stayed all day to see the big procession. The little flute band led off from the church. Then religious clubs with their uniforms from the Middle Ages marched behind, singing their special songs. Long lines of people followed, carrying huge candles almost a meter long. They sang, too, but not together. The priest came next, pulling a cart with a box to collect offerings. Everybody stretched up to catch a glimpse of the huge, beautifully dressed statue. It was in a dress like brides wear, covered with beads and lace. A team of twelve men carried the heavy weight on their shoulders, staying carefully in step so it wouldn't topple. Every three blocks they paused to let a couple of the carriers change places. The backup carriers marched right in back, ready to move in if somebody couldn't go on. Flower-bearers at each corner of the statue's platform carried large bouquets high up on poles.

After the statue came the politicians and officials wearing their sashes and waving stiffly to show how important they were. Our mayor had disappeared with the other Fascists when Mussolini died, so two of the secretaries from the town office walked in his place to represent our town. Finally came the orchestra, a concert band with almost 100 musicians all carrying their instruments and playing as they went. Conversano had the best band. Everybody knew that. Even if we weren't celebrating the end of a war, people would have traveled from all over the province to hear them.

"I'm giving my chain from *Nonna* to the Virgin," Mamma said. "It's only right to thank her for ending the war. When the procession passes, I want you to follow until they stop. Then give that necklace to the priest so he can hang it on the statue."

When the marchers stopped, I pushed through the crowd to the priest. "This is for the *Madonna*," I said, holding up Mamma's necklace. He pulled a little stool off the offering cart, climbed up, and hung the chain on the statue's hand. Several chains were there already, and she had others around her neck. Some people had pinned money to her dress and she had several brooches on her chest. People were so thankful that the war was over, they wanted to show how they felt.

According to Mamma, if you pray and ask, you have to give thanks afterward. "Even God expects payback," she said.

After the procession ended up back at the church and the statue was put back in place, the fun started. Booths around the *piazza* sold food. The delicious aroma floated through the air all the way to the church, and people followed their noses to the vendors. They had grilled sausage, loaves of bread, and cheese. Grilled *ghimerelli* made from pieces of liver and lung were roasted on a grill. One stand had more than ten kinds of olives. Under a canvas shelter, women sold cookies from a table. Men were roasting a goat on a spit above a big charcoal grill, and you could buy meat sliced off as each side became cooked. Another grill had octopus and squid. Anything you could want. It really was a feast.

There was other selling going on, too. Horses and sheep and even six chickens in cages were for sale. A kid was selling three rabbits in a little pen. Secondhand clothes hung under a tent and women were bargaining over them. People sold garden tools, ladders, buckets, and harnesses—anything you might need. I passed two men trying to outbid each other for a pair of boots with rubber coating. Nobody had seen any rubber since I was small. It was all used to make tires for the military.

Late in the afternoon the fireworks show started with a loud bang, as loud as a bomb. In a field toward the edge of town, the fireworks team had laid out all kinds of displays and they set them off in order, starting from smallest until the very loudest deafened our ears at the end. Towns always competed to see which one had the best and loudest and most organized, and the competition was fierce.

Finally as night fell, the *illuminazione* were

turned on. Electricity in the towns was still not dependable, so electricity to the houses was all turned off to allow for the decorations. The whole *piazza* was surrounded by arches and fantastic shapes formed from thousands of tiny lights. It was the prettiest sight I had ever seen. The band stood in the middle and played all the best songs from the best operas.

They ended with the national anthem, the real one, written when Italy became a nation and not *Giovinezza*, the Fascists' song. We all had to learn that one in school and sing it at *Balilla* meetings by government order. Nobody wanted that song any more. Finally we walked slowly back to the bus and went home. What a day. A day to never forget as long as I live. I wondered if they had feasts in America.

Chapter 17
Summer 1945

Mamma was a sucker for books and school. Once the war ended, life started back to normal. We had lost over a year and most of us didn't remember much about reading and writing. I still could do math, though. I kept in practice by spying on the olive buyers for Mamma and running my vegetable business.

"Are you going to go back to school?" Dominic said one day. "My father says I don't have to go any more. They can't make me go after 4th grade."

"Mamma would kill me. She stopped after 4th grade and she didn't forgive her mother yet! She wants me to be a businessman and wear a suit. Keep my hands clean. Show off in front of her friends."

"If you make lots of money you can just pay somebody to do all that stuff," Dominic said. "Let them sit in the office getting ink on their fingers and making their eyes red. It's not for me, that life."

"I can't get out of it, Dominic. I just have to put up with her until I get to America."

"You're going to America? You keep saying that. When? How can you manage it?"

"I'll think of something. I'll just go to school until I get my plan finished. Then you'll see who is smart around here."

Work came first, though—almonds late in the summer, then grapes, then olives—then school. If we didn't eat, we couldn't learn much. Almonds were the first crop and gathering them was strenuous work. We laid big canvas sheets out under the trees. Then people climbed up on ladders to shake the nuts off the branches. But those nuts were not ready to eat. The outside soft shell had to dry up and fall off. Then the hard shell had to be cracked before you could get at the nut. From the sheets, the nuts were gathered up in big bags and we took them home to spread out on the cement floor to dry.

Once they were dry, everybody helped to rub the outer shells off. We got blisters on our fingers. It was work that boys and girls could do and so they gave most of that job to us. Rosa and Mamma worked at it too until their fingers gave out. The cleaned nuts were put back into big 100 kilo bags and stored until it was time to take them to market. We kept one sack for ourselves. Most of the holiday treats would be made out of almonds, cooked, ground up, roasted, made into cakes and cookies.

"I wonder what's going on in Rome," Rosa said to Mamma one day while we sat around the mat shelling nuts. "The news on the radio says the

Americans have taken over there and that the Nazis are gone. But they don't say what is happening to the people who live there. It's only a train ride away over the mountains, but it might as well be at the end of the earth."

"That's the hardest part. Not knowing," Mamma said. "The worry fills up your head and it's hard to think of anything else. I haven't had letters from America since the war started. Do you have anyone in Rome at all?"

"No, I'm all alone."

"But surely there are cousins, godparents...no? Here we are all connected somehow."

"I wrote to my old boss, Borgati the jeweler, as soon as the Americans liberated Rome, and a letter came back through *Don* Silvestro last fall saying that over a thousand people had disappeared and had not come back. Since then, nothing. We're having another harvest and still no word. I wrote again to the jewelry shop, but that letter just came back marked 'deceased'."

"You'll get another job. Don't worry about losing your boss."

"I may not find one like Borgati. He was truly good. Before the raid, the Nazis came to the Jewish community and said we could save ourselves if we would collect enough gold for them. They wanted 50 kilograms, 110 lb. That was an impossible amount. The deadline was thirty-six hours. Everyone scraped desperately among their things to find anything of value—rings, wedding gifts, money for sure. Borgati gave a lot, even though he isn't Jewish. I heard that even the Pope sent some gold through a secret messenger. Finally we had the total, and everyone gave a sigh of relief. We were saved."

"But you had to run away. What happened, if you were saved?"

"They deceived us. On October 18, early in the morning, the SS troops came in, grabbed the people and wrecked the place. What savages. They even burn books. It's bad enough they destroyed the people, but the books contain all our knowledge. All the wisdom we have accumulated over hundreds of years. That's why I've almost given up on ever seeing Primo again. He was a book seller, a lover of knowledge. Oh, Lucia." Her voice caught in her throat.

I couldn't stand to watch Rosa cry so I pretended I had to go to the bathroom and ran upstairs. I left Mamma to comfort her if she could. There was nothing I could do.

When the weather cooled a bit we picked the grapes. Again, everyone went out into the fields including children and old people. School closed for the harvest. Each worker got a scissors or clipper and went down his assigned row clipping the big bunches of ripe grapes and putting them into baskets. Even *Nonna* Claudia came out and worked down a row. We carried the full baskets over and dumped them into a cart, then went back for more. Workdays were traded. One day's work for one day's work and people really kept track. If you needed more workers than you had friends, you had to hire people to help. At lunch, we'd have a sort of picnic, eating dry bread with tomatoes or anchovies, and then go back to work until it got dark.

Making the grapes into wine was more

complicated. First, the grapes were pressed, stems and all, in the town winepress. That juice was put into barrels until it fermented from the natural yeast found outside on the vines. After it fermented, the grape juice was siphoned off into other barrels to age for a few months in cold damp cellars. Finally it turned little by little into wine and then it was time to fill up all the bottles and put in the corks.

Everything we did took a whole team of people and it was hard dirty work. But *Nonno* was very proud of his wine. It was clear, dark red, a little sour and a little sweet. People drank it at almost every meal, a habit they learned long ago when it wasn't safe to drink the water. Even the children got some wine with water to thin it out, hoping that the wine would purify the water.

We all helped with the olive harvest too, by spreading big canvas sheets under the trees and knocking the olives out of the trees with sticks. Skinny climbers like me were sent up to shake the branches at the top. Everybody helped by taking turns at each farm so all the harvest could be done. Mamma and Rosa carried baskets to the carts with the other women.

Men drove the horse carts full of olives one by one to *u' trapitto*, the grinding mill. Each farmer's share was weighed. It was dumped into a big stone grinding press. A tired-looking horse walked round and round, pulling the handle of the huge stone wheel. The oil ran down a trough and through a screen into barrels. What came out was measured. Then they figured out each one's share, loaded the barrels back on the carts, and brought them home to store in sheds or basements until they were sold at market. We kept some of *Nonno*'s harvest in our storage because we had lots of room now that we lived upstairs again.

Children worked with their parents and neighbors, and sometimes some of the women cooked to feed the whole group. By the time the harvest was done, I was happy to sit at a school desk for a couple of months and not lift anything heavier than a pencil.

Every morning that I was free from the farm, I went until 1 o'clock to the regular school and practiced reading and writing and math. Then after lunch Mamma sent me to *dopo scuola* to learn some more from a tutor. As soon as the mail from America started, *Papá* sent us some nice cloth, American money and pasta. Mamma wouldn't get a ball for me, but she had a way to pay for what she wanted. She gave gifts from *Papá* to my teacher to ensure my good grades. With so much school, I hardly had any time for my cigarette business.

Life went on this way all that fall. We got up early to milk the goat and feed the animals in the basement, then on to school. Paper was still scarce, so we wrote very small and neat on both sides. Messing up the writing brought a smack on the hand with a ruler. So did making math mistakes, spelling words wrong, talking in class, dropping things that made noise, chewing gum, on and on. My hand was sore a lot.

Signorina Carlino told us things we had to know and wrote the important ideas on the dark-gray chalkboard. Sometimes she'd draw a map and we had to copy it into our notebooks. Other times she read poetry to us, or speeches by famous people and we had to write them down and memorize them. She read stories about ancient times or tales from the Bible. There were no stories about Mussolini, though, since the *partigiani* killed him last spring. The people who still liked him were keeping their mouths shut.

Dopo scuola was nicer because *Signorina* would laugh or tell a joke. The students in that class were all different sizes and it was like doing homework in her basement. Yes, that's right, the *Signorina*, the same teacher. The government paid her to teach in the mornings, and the parents paid her to teach in the afternoons. Either that or they brought her gifts. Her house got quite pretty, with extra vases, new tablecloths and silverware. She always wore nice jewelry to class, real gold earrings and a big shiny medal on a chain.

Mamma told me I should grow up to be a businessman or a professor or something like that. Something that would make her hold her head up in front of her friends, amaze them if possible. She said she dreamed of the day that that stuck-up Carmela, with her son the bookkeeper in the city, would see me parading through town in a suit with my shoes shiny and my professional books under my arm. After all the harvesting work I began to think she was on to something.

Chapter 18
Fall-Winter 1945

Nothing much happened the rest of that fall. After the excitement of V.E. Day and the feast, we got back to school and back to work. Mothers kept cooking and taking care of families. *Nonna* Paola and *Zia* Nina kept on making sheets and pillowcases and tablecloths on her special sewing machine.

It was called *punt' a giorno* or "stitch a day" because it went a little more than a stitch a second. You could count "one elephant, two elephant" about that fast. *Nonna* Paola did beautiful work though, and all the girls wanted her to make the sheets and things that they needed to save for their dowry, before they could be married. That work and the farm that Uncle Carlo managed kept them going.

My Uncle Carlo had a hard time working the farm, though, ever since he gave up on the war and walked home from Sicily. He had bad memories, he said, and wouldn't tell us any more. He wouldn't talk much, and got mad easily, always ready to fight. And then he'd cry and drink more wine and go to sleep.

Nonna Paola never forgave her three older boys for going off to America as teenagers and leaving her. My Uncle Carlo wasn't much help and she carried the worries of the family on her narrow shoulders.

With the poison gone from the port, more fishermen were going out to sea. Once again boats were pulled up all along the beach with nets drying over their bows. Most of the mines in the harbor were gone, so it was easier to get fish. We walked the 9 km from home to the waterfront to buy them. They sold fresh octopus and squid, mussels, and even sea urchins. They smacked the dead octopus on the stone pier over and over to make it tender.

Octopus was delicious, roasted over a fire or put into sauce. The tiny ones were good with lemon juice too. And mussels, how I loved to slurp them out of the shells. It was nice to have fish after all the *ceci*, navy beans and *fave* we ate during the war.

My vegetable business slowed down once the weather cooled off. Joe and Sgt. Thorton kept on buying vegetables as long as *Nonno* and I would sell them. Every time their ship was in port, they'd buy up our tomatoes, lettuce, Swiss chard, green beans, and peppers. When it got colder they ate up the beets and spinach and arugula. Late figs were a big seller and before Christmas it seemed that we'd be moving on to oranges. You'd think they never had fresh vegetables before. They couldn't get enough. *Nonno* was happy with his boots and socks and toothpaste.

Mamma was pleased to have soap. And I was happy with my secret stash of dollar transportation fees that I kept hidden in the old sofa.

My Uncle Antonio was a surveyor, the second most educated man in our town. He had the only radio in town and everyone respected him. He talked my mother into letting me apply for *Scuola Media* in Bari. He believed I could start right after Christmas. Our school stopped at fourth grade and most people thought that was plenty. Mamma was thrilled to have me continue—a son who would be educated and not ignorant like most others.

On a Monday morning he walked over to our house to meet with me. I was all dressed up in my *papá*'s old suit that Mamma had made small, with my shoes dusted off and my hair brushed down flat. We rode the bus into Bari, bumping over the bomb-pitted roads.

At the middle school we sat in the principal's outer office on his hard wooden chairs, smelling his cigar through the inner door and listening to his secretary's tapping on the typewriter. Finally the door opened. *"Entrate,"* he commanded. "Enter!"

We sat down on two hard chairs across from his desk. He shoved some papers across the desk to my uncle. "Fill these out: name, surname, address, age, father's occupation." He re-lit his cigar and leaned back in his chair, watching us.

Z'Antonio gave me a cautious look, took out his pen, and neatly filled in a line marked *Occupazione*: "Businessman, in America." I was confused, but I knew from his look that I should keep quiet.

"A businessman, I see. That's good," said the principal, peering over my shoulder. "We have so many ignorant *contadini* trying to get their boys in here. Now that the war is over, you would be surprised at the nerve of these people, always trying to get ahead, when their shoes still smell like a farm. But I think this boy will do nicely. His grades are good and he's nice and clean. Seems like a good family."

He pulled out his big handkerchief and gave his long nose a good blow. "The school is public as you know, but the teachers can always use a little help. He will start right after Christmas. Here is a list of supplies and books to provide. *Arrivederci.*"

He gave us his cold smile, shook hands with Antonio and waved toward the door. Out we went, feeling as though we were expected to bow.

We bought the supplies in the city that same day, and I prepared myself for Mamma's outburst. But there wasn't any outburst. She was happy, thrilled. She was willing to buy as many books as I wanted. Paper? No problem. Ink? Fine. Even bus fare. "You won't want to show up with dirty shoes." I never knew she had such a soft spot for education. I guess she really wanted me to make our family look good. I hoped I could live up to her dreams.

Chapter 19

December 1945

In the middle of December *Nonno* started
to build the *presepio*, the Christmas crèche, at his
house. He cleared a big space in the main room and
put an old table against the wall. He used cardboard
to shape a landscape, and put papier maché over
it to form little hills and valleys. He painted it and
then added tiny buildings and branches to serve as
trees. In the center he put a stable to hold the Holy
Family and baby Jesus statues. He kept adding
statues—shepherds, milkmaids, sheep, camels, girls
with ducks, boys with goats. A figure dressed in
what looked like fur represented John the Baptist.
There was a whole band of musicians with horns and
bagpipes. The Three Magi had their servants and
animals. A tiny shop held a wine seller and his little
barrels, and another had a blacksmith.

Nonno hung up a piece of dark blue cloth on

the wall behind the scene, and cut out tiny stars from a Spam can to glue on the cloth. The biggest star hung right over the stable. You could stare at it for a while and picture the whole Christmas story. On Christmas, neighbors would visit each other's homes to see what each household had created, and share a cookie or two.

As we started to talk about Christmas, Rosa grew quiet. Not that she talked that much anyway. She was a quiet person. You could see that she was educated and *istruita* because she was very polite and took turns to talk. She read all the books we had and if I brought any home from school she read those, too, right away. One time she showed me on a map where Rome was and I could see that it was a long train ride from here.

"Why are you so sad?" I asked her finally. "This is a good time of year. It's going to be Christmas. It's a lot of fun and parties and cookies."

"I'm remembering a holiday I used to have," she said. "We called it Hanukkah. It lasted for eight days and we lit one candle every day to remember," her lip trembled and she got tears in her eyes. "To remember things from long ago. It was a holy time. My mother would light one more each night and say a prayer."

"We can do that," I said. "Candles are good for all the holidays. I'll see what I can do. I have some business friends." I gave her a sly wink as if I knew what I was doing. Next day I casually asked Dominic, "Who has candles here? Can I get some?"

"Why? What for? Is your wiring down again? You use too many lights. Too much reading and homework."

"No, just some candles to make the house look good for Christmas. You know, surprise Mamma and Rosa. Women like that stuff."

At home I asked Rosa, "How many candles do you need for a holiday? Three? Four?"

"I need eight, maybe one extra. One for each day and one to light them with."

"You mean this holiday goes on for a whole week? Do the candles have to match?"

"That would be nice, but it's probably too hard for you."

"You'd be surprised what I can do. Just give me some time." I asked Sgt. Thorton and he got me three from a friend at the hospital. Joe found two in the bottom of a locker on his ship. Dominic stole one from a shop. I bought two from a friend of Angelina's. Eight altogether. She should have had more faith in me.

"Here they are Rosa. Ta da!" She looked up, surprised at my hoard. I laid them out proudly on the table.

"Three white candles, two red ones, slightly bent, one blue from Dominic and two taller yellow ones that I bought. We can put them all in a row. I'll make little holders and put them on the dining room table. You can have your holiday."

"You are the best boy I know," she cried. "You have a great heart. Your life will be a blessing." She hugged me tight. "Lucia," she said to my mother, "Your son is a treasure. A blessing!"

"If you say so," Mamma murmured, looking up from her sewing. "But don't let it go to your head, Peppino. Nobody's perfect."

"We need a little candle to light them with," Rosa had said, "to do it really properly."

"Can we get the one from in front of *Papá*'s picture? Just borrow it?" I asked Mamma. "Just for a minute?"

"One prayer is as good as another. I don't think *Papá* would mind." Mamma reached up, took it and handed it over.

So every suppertime for eight days, Rosa lit a candle—one the first night, two the next, until they were all lit. Rosa said her prayer, and we said grace and then we ate. It was nice to have an extra holiday, just when nothing else was going on.

On Christmas Eve we went to *Nonna* Paola's house. We could smell the delicious steam from her cooking as we got near. She made a feast of *frutti di mare* (oysters, mussels, sea urchins) and *baccalá* (stewed salt cod). There was a roasted *capitone* and little tiny raw squid called *calamari*. Rosa couldn't eat some of them but she loved the *baccalá*. No meat was allowed that day. That's why we had a fish party. At midnight we went to church and then home to sleep.

Christmas Day the party was at *Nonno*'s and *Nonna* Claudia's, and Rosa went with us. All the cousins were there and *Nonna* Claudia had made a big feast. As we all sat around her long table, she brought out one dish after another.

She had chicken soup with tiny meatballs, pasta with our tomatoes that we had bottled in the summer, roasted rabbit, pickled wild onions, roasted lamb, olives from our trees, spinach salad from the garden. There were artichokes fried in oil. Everybody drank *Nonno's* new wine. They passed around *finoc-chio* to take away the taste of the meats.

Then there were cookies filled with figs, dates, some made completely from almonds, some fried with fig syrup on top. We were all so full and happy to be together.

After we ate, the cousins gathered and we played *tombola* and nibbled on nuts that we cracked open. *Nonno* roasted chestnuts in the fireplace. We sang *Tu Scendi dalle Stelle*, You Come Down from the Stars, my favorite Christmas song.

Later in the afternoon people stopped in to see the *presepio*, and then we went to see theirs. People marveled at our shiny metal stars, not knowing how we had made them. There were cookies at every house, all different. After the hungry wartime, sweet treats were like a gift from heaven.

Chapter 20
January 1946

Making the family look good at school turned out to be harder than I expected. The teacher was *Don* Cirillo and he was tough, serious and picky. He was always looking for mistakes. His left arm was in a black sling but he made good use of his right one, swinging his ruler. When he looked down at me over his glasses, I shivered in my seat. Compared to him the *Signorina* was sweet. He had fought the Nazis and Mussolini with the *resistenza*, so he felt putting up with hardship and torture was part of a good education.

Most of the boys lived in nice houses in the city. They wore three or four different suits and their shirts were ironed. They talked about their vacations and their fathers' cars. It was hard for me to keep lying, but I did the best I could.

"My father owns a candy factory in America,"

I told them. "He has two cars and his house has two bathrooms. He eats meat every day." The last comment wasn't a good plan, because the others said, "So do we," and that ended the conversation.

I had to learn Latin sayings and ancient history. The math was good because I had a lot of practice helping Mamma with the crops, but I didn't dare tell my classmates about our farm business. They were all surprised that I could figure out money problems so fast. If they knew Mamma could do them in her head even faster, they would have had a different idea of farmers. Of course liters and barrels and kilograms were simple to me, so I looked pretty good in that department.

Chapter 21

February 1946

On Ash Wednesday, as we left the church with ashes on our foreheads, *Don* Silvestro trotted after us. His robes flapped around his skinny legs and he held his broad-brimmed hat against the chilly, damp wind. "*Signora*," he called. "*Aspettate. Lucia, per favore, Aspettatemi! I ginocchi mi dolono, non posso*. Wait, please wait for me. My knees hurt. I can't run so fast."

"Mamma, *Don* Silvestro is hurrying towards us," I told her.

Mamma turned in surprise. "*Cos' è, Don* Silvestro? Can we help you? Here, just sit on this bench for a minute...You shouldn't be running at your age."

"I have to show you what came in the mail. You won't believe it. See, here's a whole packet of letters addressed to various people. One of them is

for Rosa, I mean Rachel."

"Why does her letter come to you? Is her story still secret?"

" No. My friend in the *resistenza* in Rome gathered them up and sent them on. Jews there are writing letters and just sending them out to any place they can think of, trying to find loved ones. They heard my friend had contacts in this part of the country and gave him copies to send on. He sent this whole pack to me, fourteen of them."

"You brought fourteen people here?" Mamma's mouth dropped open.

"No, no, just Rosa, but other people went to other towns. We spread them around so the Nazis wouldn't notice. I'll ask around among the other priests when I see them. But here, take this to her now. You see the postmark is from last year. It's just been going from person to person, but now it has found its target."

"We'll go straight home, Father. She'll be so pleased to hear from someone. Let me see it. Is there a return name? A return address?"

"People are still afraid to put out too much information, Lucia. They haven't forgotten the past few years. They prefer to keep a low profile. Just give it to her. If she knows the person, she'll figure it out."

I beat Mamma to the door but we both arrived out of breath. "Rosa! Rachel! You have a letter!" We both shouted at once, as the door shut behind us. She came out of the kitchen where she was cutting up vegetables for soup. "What are you saying? I have a letter? But nobody here knows my name or where I live, except you two and *Don* Silvestro!"

"Here, look. Open it up!" I was in a hurry to find out who it was from. "Read it! Read it!" She looked at the Rome postmark and the handwriting and reached for a chair. She sat down hard and looked about to faint.

"I think it's from Primo," she whispered. "I thought he was dead three years ago. I saw his bookstore on fire. They took him away." She looked numb, just sitting there shaking her head. "Read it! Read it!" I started to jump up and down and Mamma put her hand on my shoulder and pressed down hard. "Let her think, Peppino. This is a big shock. Just look at her face." She turned to Rosa. "Would you want me to read it, if your eyes are bothering you?"

"No, I can read it. Whatever the news is, it is my own fate. I will face it." She leaned closer to the light, pushed up her glasses and began to read.

Dearest Rachel,
I hope and pray that this letter finds its way to you. When the Nazis raided the ghetto I prayed that you escaped. As they herded us into the trains I watched for you and didn't see you. Even in the camps, I asked other prisoners if they had seen you and no one had. And as I watched the others waste away from hunger, or be sent off to die, I gave thanks that you weren't there and maybe you could have gotten away.
My escape and the long journey from Poland

to Rome is another story. I am in Rome
now, out of the hospital and starting to
repair my bookshop.
If you get this and you remember me,
please write me c/o my bookshop in Via
Portico d'Ottavia.
   God be with you.
Shalom,
Primo

"*O Dio Mio,*" Mamma exclaimed. "He isn't
dead. He made it back home. It's a miracle!"

Rachel was already getting to her feet as she
read, and heading toward the table where I did my
homework. Her hands trembled as she reached for a
pencil. "I have to write back immediately. I can't let
him think I'm lost any longer. Auschwitz was liberated over a year ago, and he must have been hungry,
among strangers, on his own all that time. I have to
tell him that I'm alive, too."

I had an idea. "Send him a telegram. We'll
pay for it, won't we, Mamma? Won't we? Won't we?
We can send it today and he can get it tomorrow. It's
worth it!" And so Rachel wrote her first telegram.
The price depended on the number of words, so it
was short. She showed it to me. Ten words in Italian,
basic price.

Amore Mio,
Io sono viva. Vengo subito. Grazie a Dio.
Rachel

Mamma gave me a dollar and I ran to the

telegraph office. The telegram was addressed to:
Proprietor, Bookshop, Via Portico d'Ottavia, Roma.
The telegrapher looked at the address and peered
at me under his eyeshade. "Why are you writing to
Rome?" he wanted to know.

"A friend has been found alive," I said. "We
have to answer him."

He nodded. "Good news. That's the best
kind. Most of the time it is about relatives dying.
The telegram will be delivered to the shop tomorrow morning. I'll give you your change in *lire*. My
American money is all gone."

At home, Mamma and Rachel had some *orzo*
coffee on the table in front of them and had their
heads together. "We're putting a dowry together for
Rachel," Mamma told me. "She needs some things to
start her home. Go to *Nonna* Paola and see if she has
a finished tablecloth that isn't promised to anyone,
and some napkins. Tell her I'll pay her back. I know
I have a couple of new sheets tucked away and three
new towels."

"Oh no, you don't need to do all that. You're
not my mother." Rachel put her hand over Mamma's
on the table. "You gave me a safe place and treated
me kindly. That's enough."

Mamma shook her head "No, every woman
needs to start her life out right, family or not. It's too
bad we can't get you that *braciere* from the mayor's
mother. Is it all right to tell the other women we
know?"

"I think it's safe now, with the war over. Go
ahead. Tell anyone you wish. Tell the world if you
like."

"A word to Angelina will do it. She's even faster than a telegram. And a lot cheaper."

On Friday many of the women stopped by to say good-bye to Rachel and each one brought something—a handkerchief, a dishtowel, a small hard cheese, a sweater. *Nonna* Claudia brought two candlesticks. Angelina brought a blanket with a neat patch. "I only need one," she said. It must have been all that praying that brought them together.

So that's how we came to be on the bus to Bari with Rachel on a chilly Saturday morning, loaded with bundles. Dominic went with us to help carry things and protect the women. The train would leave in the afternoon and we were determined to see that Rachel and her packages got on safely. Packages could disappear in an instant if you weren't watching.

One man kept looking at our packages and edging over toward us. We'd move a bit, and there he'd be again, just to the side. Thieves and pickpockets had started their work as soon as the shooting stopped. Anyone who looked prosperous was a target. Dominic gave him a dirty look, put his arm around Rachel, and reached into his pocket for his pruning knife. It wasn't meant for fighting, but it was sharp. He pulled it out and started checking the edge against his thumb. The man melted into the crowd. Dominic's usual tough swaggering was useful for a change. Primo had already telegraphed that he would meet Rachel at the train when it arrived in Rome. We were hoping he'd bring a sturdy friend or two.

When we heard the whistle of the train pulling into the station, there was a lot of hugging. So many people were going back to their own homes

every day, and others were leaving for Venezuela
or Argentina or America, sailing from Rome and
Naples. It seemed like everyone was going somewhere. Italy would be empty.

"Write to us, tell us how things go, tell us
about the bookstore and the jewelry shop and your
new home." We crowded around Rachel.

"I will. I will always remember you. You
are my family now. And I still have those colorful
candles, Peppino. No one else has a set quite like
them." Rachel smiled and rumpled my hair.

"Good-bye. Go with God," we said. Mamma
kissed her on both cheeks and we hoisted her and her
packages up through the train door.

The train pulled away, its whistle giving out
the long lonely sound that always made me dream
of going far away. "Lent or not," Mamma said as we
crossed the busy square in front of the train station,
"I think you boys deserve a cup of *gelato* and a piece
of *torta* before we go to the bus."

Chapter 22
March 1946

The next afternoon near the *piazza* I spotted a
mop of flaming orange hair as a jeep hurtled past me.
"Where's *Capu' russ'* going, Dominic?"

"I dunno. Every afternoon around five o'clock
he rushes out of the office like that, all shined up like
he just had a bath, jumps in a jeep and takes off. He
goes out the Via Bitritto toward Bari, like a devil was
chasing him. Then a couple of hours later I see him
walking around all smiley with lipstick on his collar. I
think he has a girlfriend in Bari."

"No. How would he get a girlfriend around
here? He can hardly talk sense. He wears those
stupid shorts with his big hairy legs sticking out. His
hair would make anybody laugh. No, that can't be it.
No Italian girl is that dumb."

"I think he does," Dominic said. "I've seen
other big guys get dopey with girlfriends. Let's ask

him tomorrow. We can hang around here, picking up
cigarettes or kicking the ball around. Then when he
comes out the door, we'll jump him."

Next day, sure enough, at 3 minutes past five
o'clock p.m. out came Sgt. Thorton at a happy trot,
heading for the jeep. His shoes were shined and
the creases in his knee-length shorts were crisp. He
smelled like soap and looked like he had just shaved.
Even his orange hair was plastered down with water.
"Hey, *Capu' russ'*. Where are you going all cleaned
up?" We cornered him by the edge of the old fort,
where the wall sticks out at an angle. "Not your
concern, young fellows, not your concern."

"Aw c'mon, Sergeant. You go every day like
this. Are you a spy or what?" Dominic said.

"Of all the bloody cheek. What a dirty thing
to say of a chap. Take it back. Are you my friends or
not? I'm really quite offended!"

"Tell us, then. What are you hiding?"

" You must keep confidence, then. There's
a nice little Kiwi sister over in Bari that I'm quite
partial to. I'm going to marry her."

"Kiwis are birds. Do you think I'm ignorant?" I said. "I go to school every day, and even
dopo scuola to learn more. My mother pays a lot. So
don't try to make a fool of me!" I spit on the street
and glared at him. "Marry some bird's sister! What
kind of fool do you think I am? Are you calling me
cretino? Think I'm stupid?"

He started to chuckle and then laughed until
his face got redder than usual. "It's the language
again, isn't it? People from New Zealand are called
Kiwis. Like you call me *Capu' russ'*. We do that, too.

'Sisters' are the ladies that take care of the wounded in hospital."

"You mean *infermiere*? Or do you mean nuns? You can't marry them. They're married to God."

"No, not nuns. So that's what you call the hospital women, *infermiere*. We call them 'sisters' because they treat people as if they were their family. My Betsy tends to the wounded in hospital and she comes from New Zealand. The Kiwis run that hospital. We're going to get married next Tuesday."

"But how can you just get married like that? Does she have all her tablecloths and sheets and towels for the house? Are your parents and family coming? Do you have a party set up? Where will you get a fancy suit?" It just didn't seem that a person could get married just like that. When my cousin got married, it took the whole family more than a year of fixing and arguing, planning and sewing, and making cookies.

"We'll just go before the Captain. My assistant will stand up. We'll say our vows and sign the book and that will be it, ten minutes at most. Betsy's to wear her nursing uniform and carry some flowers. Then back to work. We may get a three-day leave if she can find another sister to work for her. Nobody has time or money for all that ceremony."

That was the craziest wedding I ever heard of. How could they expect to stick together for a whole life if they did it so fast? It didn't make sense. "*Auguri*, I guess," I said. "Best wishes." I shrugged. Dominic said the same and we shook his hand. What could we do? The poor *fesso* was hooked.

As we walked away, "It's too easy," Dominic said. "It won't last."

The next Monday when Joe and his gang were in port, they came over to see if any of our salad was ready to pick yet. "Did you hear about the wedding?" I asked.

"Who's getting married?" Joe said. "Not me."

"Yeah, you're too young and too smart," added Art. "Now I myself might give it some thought if I find a pretty girl who's willing." He rubbed his hairy cheeks and pulled in his belly. "Just haven't found the right one yet, that's all."

"You mean they've all said no," Joe laughed. "You don't exactly have to fight the girls off, you know. What's the story, Peppino?"

"It's Sgt. Thorton. He's marrying a girl from New Zealand next week. It's a fast wedding."

"Ah, a Kiwi?" Art said. "Them Kiwis, now. They're tough. You know they fought all across Africa and almost drove out Germans out of there. Then the Allies sent 'em here to take care of casualties. And they're full o' the devil, don't you know, telling jokes and making everybody laugh even when it hurts. I met a wounded guy, one leg all blasted and done up in bandages, leaning on a crutch. I bumped into him, don't you know, by accident and felt so bad almost tipping him over. 'So sorry' I said. 'I'm a clumsy son-of-a-gun, almost knocked off your leg.' And do you know what he told me? 'No fears, mate, I've got another.' "

"They've got guts, Art, that's for sure," Joe said." Thorton's a lucky man.

Chapter 23

Early April 1946

We didn't see much of Sgt. Thorton for a few weeks—just the back of him hurrying away in the jeep. "I guess he really likes that Betsy sister," Dominic said one day.

"I don't get it," I said. " She's just a girl even if she does dress up in that blue and white hospital dress and have cute dots all over her face. I don't see why he has to hang around her all the time."

"You'll see when you're older. The girls get prettier and all the guys change. They get together like magnets. It's automatic."

Just then Joe and his friends came by. "We don't have any vegetables yet, Joe. It's been too cold even for spinach. Maybe we'll have some arugula next time you're in port."

"There won't be a next time, kid. We just got new orders. Once we leave here we have to go to the shipyard and they're going to refit the ship to carry passengers. Our new orders are to carry troops back home. We'll carry refugees too, to any place that will take them. Argentina, Australia-- America for some."

"You won't be coming back? Not ever?"

"Only if I come on vacation, and I don't think I'll ever afford a vacation like that. All the world I'll ever see will be from the deck of a troop ship."

"Do you want to meet my family before you go? I could ask Mamma."

" We already know your grandpa. How many more relatives do you have?"

"Just Mamma and me at our house, but then there are cousins, and my godparents and—"

"I get it," Joe laughed. "My family is like that, too. It goes on forever and everybody is connected."

"If she says OK, will you come? Will you be here the rest of the week?"

"Sure, we'll come. Won't we, boys?" Art and Popeye nodded vigorously. "Will she make spaghetti and meatballs?"

"Better than that. You'll see! I'll tell you tomorrow. Do I have to come to the port?"

"That would be better, yeah. Come to the port. We'll show you the ship. We're supposed to stay close in case they need more help loading supplies or moving things around. They're putting in new radio equipment that needs careful handling."

At supper I asked Mamma casually, "How do you feel about a party, Mamma?"

"A party? What feast is it? How many people do you want to bring?"

"Just Joe and his friends. They've been good

customers and they're never coming back." I told
her about their new orders. "I promised to tell them
tomorrow at the port. They're going to show me their
ship."

"You seem to think you own this family,
now that you believe you're a businessman. But I
don't mind feeding a few people. They've been very
decent with us and, of course, Joe is Italian, even if
his family lives in New Jersey and his language is
terrible."

"How about *Capu' russ'* and his new wife?
He's a friend, too, and they didn't have any wedding
party. Remember? They had to go right back to work.
And of course, *Nonno* and *Nonna* Claudia, *Nonna*
Paola and Dominic—"

"Just stop the list right there. This table only
holds ten and all those men will eat a lot. If they can
come Sunday afternoon, I'll do it, but I'll have to start
right away."

"No cousins?"

"No cousins! We're not starving, but we're not
rich. And I can't expect them all to bring food like
we do for family. No, just a small party, ten counting
you and me. That's my final offer. When you go to the
port tomorrow, bring me back a nice octopus, about
a kilo in size. No, wait, make that two. And some sea
urchins and mussels and oysters. I'll make *frutti di
mare*."

"That's it? Just fish?"

"Of course not! But we have most of what we
need right here from the farm. *Nonno* will help with
meat, I know. And maybe I can get *Nonna* Claudia to
bake something."

The next morning I set off early for Bari. The nine kilometers walk went fast as I scurried along with the promise of touring the ship at the top of my mind. Mamma had given me three American dollars to bargain with, and a list that included mussels and squid along with the octopus. "First tell them you only have a dollar," she said. "Say they don't look all that fresh, start to walk away. Then if they call you back, say you have a little money of your own if they can add another handful of mussels. You know how to do it. You've watched me since you were a baby."

I bought the fish and watched as the fisherman pounded the octopus on the stone. Once it was nice and tender, I talked him into keeping it all on his block of ice until I would come back. I told him I had business with the Americans and might be able to send him some customers. "They love fish," I told him. "That's how Americans are—fish in the morning, fish for supper, they can't get enough. That's why they sail the sea." He smiled. Either he believed me, or he thought I was funny. It's hard to tell sometimes with grownups.

Once I found the ship, the guard wouldn't let me on. He said even children can't go on without a pass, especially children. Joe came up from his work and asked him in English, but he still wouldn't change his mind. "Get back to duty, sailor," he barked. "You know it's against regulations."

"Sorry, Peppino," Joe said. "We'll see you Sunday. What time?"

"After church. When you get there. Dinner time. Just use your head," I replied.

Loaded with fish and other "invertebrates,"

as my teacher calls them, I walked home. The fish seemed to weigh a ton and the longer I walked, the slower I got, with salt water dripping out of my cloth bag and leaving a trail. A couple of cats followed me, but I chased them away. I didn't need that kind of company. I heard of a town in the north with the nickname of *mangiagatti* because they ate cats when they were starving. These cats were safe from me.

As I passed the *municipio* I stopped in at Sgt. Thorton's office to invite him and *Signora* Betsy. "A generous offer, my boy, most generous. We shall be happy to attend. Betsy has been amongst the sick so long she scarcely knows what good food tastes like."

Next day, as soon as I came home from school, Mamma had jobs for me. "You don't think a party makes itself, do you? And now that Rachel's gone back to Rome, you're the helper here."

Almonds were my first job. The inner shells had to be broken to take out the nuts. Then Mamma boiled them to remove the brown skins. She drained them and passed them back for me to grind them up into paste with the hand grinder. I brought the big bowl of the almond paste to *Nonna* Claudia. She added eggs and sugar and lemon to make pasta reale, an almond cake like marzipan.

As soon as I got back home with the almonds, I got sent to *Nonna* Paola to borrow some hard wheat flour for the pasta. Mamma wanted to make *orecchiette*. That means "little ears." She shaped them one by one with her fingers, a few hundred at least. I brought up tomatoes in jars, olives in jars, pickled wild onions, dry onions, spices, more oil. Then she wanted any salad I could find in the garden, so it was off to hunt for spinach and arugula that had made it through the winter. This party was a lot of work and we still had two days to go. I was happy to sit in class the next morning just to get a bit of rest.

Mamma kept going the next day, putting out the good tablecloth with *Nonna* Paola's sewing all around it. She washed all the dishes again in the new sink, and polished up the glasses. *Nonno* killed three rabbits and a chicken. They sent me to buy lamb neck bones at the *macelleria*. It was looking like a feast, after all.

At church on Sunday all I could think of was the party. With the house ready, all we had to do was wait but we didn't have to wait long. Joe and Art and Popeye arrived first, followed by *Nonno* and the two grandmas. Dominic came running in, only to be stopped by Mamma at the door and told to go wash up and put on a clean shirt if he planned to eat at her table.

Sgt. Thorton and Betsy arrived a bit late. He wore his dress uniform with more medals than I ever knew about. Betsy wore her blue uniform dress with a crisp white apron and a tidy white hat. Her face was round and smiling, with those cute tan dots around her nose. Her brown hair was rolled up and pinned firmly in place.

"Sorry to be behind time," he said. "My wife Betsy, here, was working with a patient and he turned sour. She didn't have time to change."

"You have a sour patient? How can that be?" I asked. It didn't make sense.

Betsy explained, "He got sicker. In fact we may lose him altogether. He has an infected wound and if we could get that new medicine, penicillin, perhaps he'd make it," Betsy said. "He's resting and that's all we can do. Give him a place to rest and hope nature heals him."

By this time Joe had followed his nose into the kitchen. "It smells like I died and went to heaven, Mrs. B," he said. "I mean, *Signora*. I mean, *il profumo è molto bello*."

"What is he saying, Peppino? Help me understand. Can you explain us all to each other?"

"I'll try, Mamma. We'll just have to wave our hands a lot and smile. I get some of the words, but not all. Joe gets some, too. *Capu' russ'* still needs his little book and it's really slow. I don't know about Betsy."

"Well, food doesn't need translation. Call them all to the table."

And so we ate. We ate thin slices of sausage and cheese. Then we had fresh oysters and sea urchins with lemon juice. Then came the octopus in a tomato stew. The guests were looking a bit full, so I told Joe, "You have to take your time, this is only the beginning. You tell them, Joe: *piano, piano*."

When they heard that, his friends eyes opened wide and they looked around. They didn't see any more food. Betsy loosened her white belt by one notch. Sgt. Thorton unbuttoned his jacket. *Nonno* just smiled. Mamma served us each a small bowl of golden chicken broth "to clear our stomachs."

Then she came in with the big dishes of *orecchiette al sugo*. Everybody ate a dish of that with grated homemade cheese from our goats on top. After that came the roasted rabbit and salad and pickled onions and a dish of our own olives. "I'm sorry to have such a skimpy dinner," Mamma said, "but the war has made it hard to find things."

"Skimpy! We're fed like hogs for slaughter," said Sgt. Thorton. "Henry the Eighth couldn't have eaten better. I don't think I've ever had a meal like this."

"Maybe we should talk a while before dessert, then," Joe said. "Mrs. Thorton, I hear you are a nurse. Were you working at the hospital when the big attack happened at the harbor?"

"I had just arrived and we were setting up our supplies. We had to sort the injured as they were brought in. If they looked sure to die, we put them in one big room and the chaplain visited. Those that seemed to have a chance, those we washed off well and gave them the medications we had. We gave them plasma for shock and tried to keep them warm. We were afraid they'd catch pneumonia from the chill. So many die from that, you know."

"What about the poison gas though? What did you do for that?"

"We didn't know about it at the time. Nobody did. When they started to get blisters all over and turn yellow we knew their problem went deeper, but no one knew how to treat them. After a couple of days one of the doctors found a medical article about nitrogen mustard poisoning. Both sides in the war had pledged not to use that poison, though, so we thought it wasn't possible. All the officials said there wasn't any. Then the patients started dying. Their bone marrow was so damaged they couldn't make proper cells, so after a few days they simply died despite our efforts. It broke our hearts to see the poor chaps suffer so." Her big blue eyes filled with tears and *Capu' russ'* pulled out his big handkerchief and handed it to her.

"We came in on the ships just afterwards, with replacements of medical supplies," Joe said. "We were loading up in North Africa, and an emergency call came in over the radio to load up as fast as possible and head straight to Bari. The harbor really stank when we came in. There were smoking hulks of ships everywhere and they were still finding bodies. The whole place smelled like garlic. You could smell it out at sea when the wind was westerly."

"*Signora* Betsy," I wanted to know, "do you know our doctor? He's always trying to learn new things. Does he come to your hospital? His name is Loconte Eduardo. We call him *Don* Eduardo." She smiled, remembering. People always liked *Don* Eduardo once they met him.

"Yes, I met Dr. Loconte. He came to a meeting about treating infections. He wanted to know about a new medicine he heard about called penicillin. He hoped to get some for his patients. We had to tell him that since it is so new and there are so many wounded, that it's impossible to get."

"We've brought in penicillin," Joe said. "They guard it like gold. Everyone who handles it has to sign a receipt so they can keep track of it. We brought drugs, bandages of all kinds, and instruments for surgery. Shiploads at a time."

"If it weren't for you sailors, we'd be in a sorry state," Betsy said. "You've been everyone's lifeline, and not always appreciated. A few heavy drinkers have given you a bad reputation. There's even been talk on the radio accusing you of dodging the draft."

"That's a stinkin' lie," Joe said. "Some weak-kneed radio commentator back home has been spreading that word. A lot of us couldn't get in the army when we tried. They wouldn't take me because of my thick glasses and the left eye that doesn't track right. Art here was too old and fat for them. Popeye had some trouble with the law when he was younger, and his record followed him. We wanted to do our bit, though, so here we are. We've been bombed and sunk as often as the combat ships."

"No one's belittling your efforts, Joe. It's just a rumor, that's all. You know there's always talk," Sgt. Thorton said. "Those who do nothing always have the most to say."

"All this serious talk will make us sad," *Nonno* said. "The war is over and we're among friends. Let's have dessert. I think I still have a little *limoncello* left over from before the war."

Nonna Claudia brought in the *pasta reale*. She had put a thin frosting over it and sprinkled pieces of almond on top—almonds on almonds. She served each guest a slice and *Nonno* put *limoncello* from his own lemon trees into tiny fancy glasses and passed them around. Everyone ate slowly now, tasting each bit of the almonds and lemons, letting every drop of the lovely flavors sink in. As we said good-bye that night a lot of the grownups had tears in their eyes. Friends were going away probably forever.

Chapter 24

Late April 1946

"Hey, Peppino," Dominic whispered as we were crossing the *piazza*. "Did you hear *Signora* di Nardi yelling last night?"

"What happened? Was she mad at one of her kids?"

"No." He ducked his head and pulled me closer. "Her husband in America has a lady friend. She smokes cigarettes and wears makeup and talks American. Angelina told her. It was in a letter she got from her cousin Tony in Chicago. *Signora* Di Nardi is going to move to America."

I couldn't believe it. In the first place, Ciccio Di Nardi was the ugliest man I knew, and he was so cheap he used to put extra water in his own home-made wine. Why would a lady who talked American even waste her time on him? But you could never doubt news that came from Angelina. She had all the news and it got even more interesting every time she told it.

"What's more," Dominic went on, "that letter said almost all the fathers in America have lady friends. That's why sometimes the money letters don't come on time. What about your *papá*? Do you think he has a girlfriend?"

That idea hit me like a punch in the stomach. Could that be possible? But *Papá* is good, Mamma says so, and lights a candle in front of his smiling picture every night before saying her prayers. He sends us American pasta and real coffee and he sent me another old suit that Mamma is making smaller for my First Communion. He's one of the few people Mamma trusts. "It's not possible," I said. "*Papá*'s honest. He wouldn't do something like that." But it gave me an idea. It would be worth a try.

I got to school early. I wanted to look at the big map and see where all my friends were from, all those places we talked about at the dinner. I never thought about it before, but I knew people from all over the world.

As I entered the classroom, I saw *Don* Cirillo at his desk, eating his breakfast. "What are you doing in here, Binetti? Have you developed a thirst for knowledge? I wouldn't have expected it, given your marks." He made a sour face and dusted some crumbs off his dark striped tie.

"*Per favore, Don* Cirillo, I wanted to look at your big map. I can't see it all from my seat. I wanted to find some places I heard about—New Zealand, England, New Jersey, Libya."

"Commendable. *Complimenti.* An interest in

geography informs the mind. That's an interesting combination of countries, Binetti. Why do you need this information? Are you planning to travel?" He peered at me over his dark-rimmed glasses.

"Not just now, Sir. I met some people during the war and wanted to see where they came from."

Don Cirillo smiled, I think for the first time ever. "That's the first intelligent remark I've heard in this classroom in a long time, an actual desire to learn. Here, let me show you." He pulled the big map down on its roller, and got out his pointer. He pointed them all out, even New Jersey, which turned out to be a little tiny smudge near the edge of America. "Is Poland far?" I asked. He gave me a piercing look. "What do you know about Poland?"

"Nothing, really. I have a friend who knows somebody who came home from there at the end of the war. Came back to Rome after he was taken away. He walked a lot. I want to know how he did that. She said he escaped at the end of the war. Escaped from what?"

"Look. Here's Poland. The war was at its worst all across here toward the end." He swung is pointer over a big wide path north of Italy. "People were being destroyed right and left. Nobody knew which side to be on. The Germans were desperate. Your friend's friend would have had to make his way south through destroyed lands, then find a ship of some kind to cross the Adriatic here to Venice or even a small town along the coast. After that he'd need to find a train or walk over a hundred miles avoiding armies and battles much of the way. It took tremendous courage or perhaps desperation." He stopped

and thought a minute. "Did you say he was 'taken'?"

"Yes. Soldiers burned down his shop and loaded people on trains."

"And you say this was the friend of your friend. Did your friend stay with you by any chance? Arrive suddenly? Have a change of name? Live a very quiet sad life?"

"Yes. How did you know? We promised not to betray her. We didn't tell anybody. She's safe now anyway. Gone back to Rome."

He gripped my shoulder. For a moment I thought he'd hug me. "Your family are the kind that make life worth the effort," he said. "The unknown decent people save the world. Remember that. Here," he said, holding out his book of maps. "You can borrow this for a week. Just be sure to bring it back. Look up all the places you want to learn about. You can draw the shapes in your notebook to help you remember. Maybe some day you'll see one of them in real life. Now, go to your seat. The other boys are coming in." That was the longest and friendliest talk I ever had with him.

French, though, was still a nasty subject. I couldn't get my mouth around those sounds. I sounded to myself as if I had a terrible cold, and the other kids laughed and mimicked me. It was miserable. And when would I ever meet any French people anyway? Everybody here talked English or American or some kind of Italian. It was just some kind of scheme to keep the teachers busy, I thought.

I also learned other things from those city boys that weren't in the books. I heard stories about fathers having extra girlfriends and even other families. Stuff about boys and girls playing around together. Some bad words. They showed some pictures around that Mamma wouldn't have liked. I was a quick learner. I started to think that maybe I could make that "businessman" thing really work out as long as it didn't involve France.

"Mamma," I said one day late in the spring, "Do fathers always have extra girlfriends?"

"*Che vergogna*! Shame on you!" she snapped. "Where do you get such ideas? Fathers are loyal to their families. At least most of them are. *Papá* is a saint." I just smiled a little smile and said, "Of course, Mamma, *certo*." But I could see a wave of worry go across her face.

I waited a week or so and mentioned that Mimmo di Nardi had told me that his mother was going to move to America to save his father from a person she called *la puttana*. They were going to go on a ship after Christmas. Mamma frowned, pressed her lips together and turned to drain the pasta. "She shouldn't call anyone a name like that," she said. "Di Nardi isn't such a great prize himself." She shook the drainer a couple of extra times and set it down hard. Nothing more was said.

When my first report card came home with all *lodevoli*, highest honors. Mamma was very happy. She wasn't so happy with the news that *Don* Cirillo was hinting that his silverware was very old, and that the price of oil and pasta were much too high. We knew what that meant. More "voluntary contributions" were expected if I wanted to see any more *lodevoli*. Just because he loaned me his book didn't change that. Business was business.

"Dominic says his cousin wrote that schools in America are free. You don't have to give presents to get good grades," I said casually. "...up through high school. That's what they call *Liceo*. They say some universities are almost free, too. He heard American soldiers talking about studying to be lawyers and doctors at a university when they get home. Joe wants to learn to be an accountant and work in a bank." I dropped all this casually, like I just didn't care.

Mamma was quiet for a moment and then recovered. "What do we care? We have a beautiful house here, and land, and some day your *Papá* will come back. Go do your homework." I could hear the doubt in her voice though. Maybe I could plant some gossip with Angelina. She'd love to have something new to think about. But what if Mamma got so mad at *Papá* that she wouldn't go? I dropped that plan. Yet it was just stupid for us to stay here guarding trees and eating rabbits when we have friends all over the world, I thought.

Later that week Mamma said, "We have to talk seriously. After supper. Your father has sent a letter. To you, yourself, not to me." Well, that was something new. He never wrote to me before. He wasn't much of a writer, even to Mamma.

After the dishes were washed, we sat down at the table. She pulled her chair up tight on her side, put her elbows up and propped her chin in her hands. Her face was serious and worried. Something was going to happen—I could feel it. "This has your name on it—Binetti, Giuseppe—and that doesn't mean *Nonno*. Open it."

I tore it carefully. What could be so important? After all these years, after almost all my life, *Papá* sends me a personal letter. I wasn't sure he remembered I was even alive, yet he did send me his old suits. A puzzle.

"Read it, Peppino," she said. "You're a good reader now, *tu sei istruito*. Put those expensive lessons to use. You probably read and write more than *Papá* and me put together. See what he says."

I read silently:

Mio caro figlio Peppino,
   Congratulations. You will soon be twelve and almost a man. I have a home here in Chicago. I saved up enough money that our family can be together. Your mother loves her land and her home, but a family belongs together. Now that you are a man, I give you a man's responsibility. Make her come to America. In her last letter, she said that she trusts you now, and says you are "Buon' com' il pane." That is great praise. You know your mother never praises anyone. Convince her to come. Do what you have to do.
   Baci—e Coraggio!
   Papá

"What is it?" Mamma said. "What does he want? What does he write in secret to you and not to me?" She looked at me suspiciously.

"He wants us," I replied. "He wants us all to be together, in America." In my mind I could see that big map with America over on the left side colored pink.

"You mean leave all that we have to go away? Leave this house behind? Leave our olive fields? That's a crazy idea." She was gathering her voice and working up to a storm.

"*Calma, Mamma! Calma!* Settle down! *Papá* loves us. He wants us. He said I'm to be the man of the house now."

Mamma took a deep breath and glared at me. I could see this was going to be like wrestling those rocks out from under the olive trees. But *Papá* said I should do it. He believed in me. "*Papá* said, "I told her. "He has a house. He wants his family in it. It's only fair. *È giusto.*"

Mamma sniffed, pressed her lips together and looked down at the table. "*Ci arrangiam',*" she said. "We'll find a way. I don't want to be like Mimmo's mother."

There was a crack in her armor already. With a little luck in a few months I'd be in America, walking on those gold streets and becoming somebody. I'd need all the *coraggio* I could muster.

Author's Notes
Peppino, Good as Bread

Most of the stories in this book actually happened. My husband grew up in a small town in southern Italy during World War II, and Peppino tells his stories and those of his friends and relatives. For example, the Fascist mayor of the town did take over my husband's family home (and install a bathroom) since it was one of the best houses. The family did live in the basement, and raise rabbits for food and goats for milk there. They did run short of food and make do with what they could get, often from the black market. They ate "weeds" that we call arugula.

The story about tricking the soldiers with empty eggs did happen, and the boy behind it was actually named Dominic. He told me his story when he was almost 80 years old.

Some people sat on their rooftops to watch bombardments. Italians love fireworks, especially the loud booms.

Most people had nicknames because their official names are duplicated over and over throughout a family. A lot of those names are not flattering. For example, the town crier's real nickname was *Vituccio u' ca caat* (poopy pants).

The town was mostly populated by women, children, and older men because the younger and middle-aged men were in one army or another. Kids helped in every way and worked very hard.

After the armistice, when Italy agreed not to fight America, there was a lot of confusion and anger among the people. Some felt betrayed. The Fascists still held power and didn't let anyone forget it. Most people hated the Nazis for the way they treated the Italian people even when they were on the same side. As the Allies -- Britain, Australia and America -- invaded Italy and spread northward through Sicily and Naples to drive the Germans out, the Germans took out their anger on the people. Around Rome and up north towards Abruzzo, there were even massacres. The Germans around Bari depended on food from the farms and the use of the harbor, so they were not as destructive of the population.

Because of the Nazi persecutions, many Jews were smuggled by Italian groups out of areas like Rome and hidden among the people in small Italian towns, so Rachel's story is true. People like her were called "*sfollati*" which means "out of the flock" because they were dispersed. They often had jobs. Some opened businesses. Even at concentration camps set up by Nazis, under Italian control, conditions were more humane. Southern Italians always disliked governmental authority and ignored as many official directives as they could get away with.

After the Germans had retreated northward, and the British controlled Bari with American
support, a solitary German pilot notified his com-
mander that ships were unloading equipment for the
Allies in the harbor at Bari. No one knew that there
was a supply of mustard gas, a chemical weapon,
secretly stored in a Liberty ship, the John Harvey,
to use in case Germany violated an agreement not
to use it. The Germans sent an air raid to destroy
the supply ships. Seventeen ships were destroyed
and the mustard gas was released. There were heavy
casualties among the military workers and the Italian
civilians. Because the poison gas was a deep secret,
no one knew how to treat the injured. The facts of
the case were only unclassified in the late 1950's. The
attack has been called "the second Pearl Harbor." In
later years the same chemical was found to be useful
in treating cancer, since it kills the blood cells.

So, the story is as true as it can be, and still
be a story. The names in the story are real, but are
attached to other people. The times and the place are,
I hope, as real as can be—the smells, the worn-out
clothes, the fear, the tricks, the loyalty, the survival.

Glossary of Italian
Words & Phrases

Word/Phrase	Meaning
al sugo	in (tomato) sauce
americani	Americans
aquedotto	aqueduct, water supply
armadio	clothes cabinet
Arrangiam'	We'll work it out
Aspetta!	Wait!
Auguri	(best) wishes
Ave Maria	Hail Mary, prayer
avere	to have
baccalá	stewed salt codfish
Baci	"Kisses" on a letter
Balilla	boys' group
banditore	town crier
biscotti	pastry with coffee
braciere	brazier
Buon'Com'il Pane	As good as bread, honest
Buon' lavoro	"Happy work"
calamari	squid
calma	calm down

camion	large trucks
Campo Sportivo	Soccer field
capisce	understands
capitone	eel
Capu' russ'	"red head"
cara	dear one
carissima	my dearest
carne	meat
ceci	chickpeas
certo	certainly
Che coglione!	What nerve!
Che fai?	What are you doing?
Che vergogna	How shameful
Che è?	Who is it?
chiami or chiam'	call, as in name yourself
chiedere	to request
ciao	hi (or) bye
cibo	food
Commar'	godmother
contadini	land workers
Coraggio	Have courage
Cosí è la vita	Life is like that
costa	(does it) cost
cretino	stupid person
del' carne	some meat
Don	honorary, man
Donna	honorary, woman

donna seria	serious woman
dopo scuola	"after school"
È basta!	That's all!
È giusto	It's fair
Entrate	Come in, formally
espresso	strong coffee
fascisti	Facist members
fave	broad beans
fesso	fool
ficcanaso	"poke her nose"
finita	finished
finocchio	anise
Fonte	fountain
forestieri	outsiders
frittate	omelets
frutta di mare	seafood
gelato	ice cream
Genoveffa	heroine of the story
gentiluomo	gentleman
ghimerelli	grilled liver or lung
ginocchi	knees
Giovinezza	Fascist song
Grazio Dio	Thanks be to god
guaglione	boy, kid
Guardia campestre	farm police
Ha ragione	"You (polite) have a point"
Hauptmann	German captain

Eee Madonna!	Exclamation
Il Duce	Mussolini, "The Leader"
il ladro	thief
il silenzo	the silence
illuminazzione	light decorations for feasts
infermiere	hospital nurses
Inglese	English
Io sono viva	I am alive
istruiti	instructed persons
kilo	1000 grams
Kommandant	Commander (german)
La Befana	good witch
La Bellino	maiden name
la borsa nera	black market
La guerra	the war
la serva	the servant, maid
Leutnant	Lieutenant (german)
Liceo	High school
limoncello	lemon liquer
lire	Italian money
lodevole	report card "A"
macelleria	butcher shop
Maledetta	cursed
mangiagatti	cat-eaters
Margarit d'u' casin'	Margaret of the fancy house
mi dolono	hurt me
Mimmo	Dominic

Mincuccio	Dominic
mio	mine
Misericordia	(Have) mercy
molto bello	very beautiful
municipio	city hall
muratore	stone mason
muscia muscia	flabby, slow, lazy
Nonno	grandpa
Nora	daughter-in-law
orecchiette	"little ear" pasta
orzo	coffee from barley
pane rustico	country bread or rustic bread
papier maché	shape of mashed paper
pasta e fagioli	pasta with beans
pasta reale	pastries like marzipan
pazzi	crazy (plural)
per disobbligare	to remove obligation
piano, piano	"slow, slow", take it easy
piazza	a paved square
podestá	mayor
Policlinico	major hospital
port' indietro	bring back, return
portone	garage-type door
posso	can (I)
poverella	poor thing, female
pozzo	rainwater tank
presepio	Christmas creche

profumo	scent, perfume
punt' a giorno	hemstitch machine
puoi	you can...
puttana	hussy
qualche	some (kind)
Quanto	How much
qui	here
rapini	vegetable
Residenza	residence
resistenza	underground
Romana	Roman woman
sacco	bag
salotto	sitting room, parlor
saurbraten	meat stew (german)
Scuola Media	Middle School
Scusi	Excuse me, sorry
sei	(you) are
speriamo	let's hope so
State zita	Stay quiet
stato pigliato	I've been taken...
strega	a witch
Stupidi	stupid (persons)
taralle	a dry pastry
Third Reich	Hitler's state
torta	cake
tu	you (familiar)
tutti	all, everybody

U' Surd'	"the deaf"
ufficiale	uniformed official
un buon' figlio	a good son
un cancello	a wrought iron gate
un momento per favore	"a moment, please"
Va Pensiero	aria by Verdi
Vai!	Go!
Vengo subito	I come right away
vero	real, true
vieni	come
villa	park in town
Vituccio	nickname for Vito
volete	do you want?
Z' Tonino	Uncle Anthony
zio	uncle
zitto	(be) silent